Xamon Song

Xamon Song

A Novel

Adam E. Stone

Global Dialogue Press   *P.O. Box 1781*   *Mt. Vernon, IL 62864*

ISBN-13: 978-0-9771396-0-6
ISBN-10: 0-9771396-0-3
Library of Congress Control Number: 2005937713

The author wishes to thank Nancy Flowers, Philip St. Clair, Charlotte Raymond, Shannon Green, Vernon A. Stone, Saribenne Evesong, Christy Hargesheimer, and Richard T. Goldstein for reading early drafts of *Xamon Song* and offering wonderful suggestions.

Global Dialogue Press is a member of the Green Press Initiative. This novel is printed on 50% post consumer recycled paper.

For my father, Vernon A. Stone
1929-2005

And for General Dallaire, who tried

It could be anywhere ... most likely could be any frontier ... any hemisphere ...

The Clash, "Straight to Hell"

WELL SO THERE WE STOOD, frozen in our tracks - listening, watching, waiting; wondering if we'd hear that sound again, that sharp, whacking sound, like a stick being snapped under a foot; or maybe a branch being popped clean off a tree; or maybe a round being chambered into a rifle or an M9 pistol; wondering if it was an animal, foraging up some food, or a local villager doing the same, or maybe, and probably more likely, someone a whole lot worse. And me wondering too how Mike had ever talked me into doing this, into joining the Carbonia Air Corps with all these crazy wars and things going on.

"They're gonna be starting the draft up again soon," he'd said, "and you know it isn't gonna be any of those rich kids they're drafting. It's gonna be people like you and me, Eddie-man, people stuck in Nyala with nothing to do and nowhere to go but into the service. And if we get drafted it's the Army, infantry even, where we'll just be big fat targets for anyone who wants to take a shot at us. At least if we join up now we can go Air Corps," he'd added, nodding his head in a knowing kind of way, smiling and making a little clicking sound out of the corner of his mouth, something he always did when he was wanting to stress what he was saying.

And far as I could figure he did seem to have a point, though I've never been the real political sort, and I couldn't have said for sure whether that whole draft thing was gonna happen or not; but Mike, he was pretty good at thinking things out, and most all the time I'd take stock in what he said, and generally he'd turn out to be right. One thing I was pretty sure about was that if there was to be a draft, it would be people like Mike and me who'd get hit up for it first, not downright poor so much as what you might call working-class, people from Nyala and other towns like it all over Carbonia, with nothing but the paper mills and the rubber works to provide a living, and not much of one at that.

Me, I'd lived in Nyala all my life, and so had Mike, and we'd been friends for as long as either of us could remember. Used to be we'd just ride our bikes around, or maybe go walking out to some of the old abandoned buildings on the rubber works property, but our plan

2

since we were about fourteen had been to start a band together, with me playing guitar and Mike singing. Mike, he was gonna write all our song lyrics too, being as how he had a natural knack for that, while me, I never have been very good at putting words together. So me, I saved up best I could and bought a cheap used guitar, fashioned to be an imitation of those pricier, more fancy ones, and a little no-name practice amp, and I took to teaching myself songs off the radio and CDs and such; yeah, and before long I took to writing some songs of my own, and Mike, he liked them, he was downright impressed with them. And me, I liked Mike's lyrics too, being as how they were fresh and what you might call exciting and energizing, not all old and worn out like so many lyrics you hear on the radio, though they could take to being a little down and negative sometimes, which was how Mike himself could take to being every now and again.

See, Mike could be pretty particular, pretty hard to please you might say, and that sometimes made him kind of rough to be around. Like with the band, like with trying to find other people to play our music with: Mike, he'd get all enthusiastic about some bass player or drummer he'd heard about, and he'd call him up and talk him into jamming with us, but then he'd always find something wrong with the guy, like maybe the guy was too worried about having the right image and looking good, or maybe partied all the time, or maybe just wasn't serious enough about making it to the top with us; and then Mike would get all downcast and sullen-like, and he'd talk on how we'd never get anywhere in Nyala, never find anyone around there who had what it takes to make it in the music business. And truth be told that was a big part of us joining up too, being as how Mike talked it up all big and major about the Air Corps being our chance to get out of Nyala, to see the world and live and meet lots of new people and have lots of new things to write our music about.

So there we were, half a world away from Nyala, on a path in a forest in a tiny country called Xamon, standing stock still and straining all our senses to try to figure out if we were about to walk into something fierce, maybe like an ambush or some other such thing. Far as we could figure from the briefings we'd been getting from our intelligence folks, the area we were in was swarming with all sorts of potential dangers, and you couldn't ever tell who was on whose side, leastways not out there smack in the middle of it. On paper, you see, we were friends with the Xamon Army, and the air base that Mike and me and the other Air Corps security forces troops were guarding was put there courtesy of the government of Xamon; but rumor had it--and our intelligence folks couldn't, or leastways wouldn't, confirm or deny this--that the Xamon Army was up to some bad stuff out there, or leastways collaborating in some bad stuff, things they wouldn't want to be seen doing, so we had to be just as careful around them as we did around the others. And the others were what you might call a pretty motley bunch themselves, them being the rebels who were fighting the Xamon Army, and the paramilitaries who were supporting the Xamon Army against the rebels, and then the local villagers, who could be supporting any of the above or no one at all, and also various other aid people and so on.

Now like I said, I'm not the real political sort, but Mike, he'd done some thinking on this, and he'd taken to trying to sort it all out, to explain to me just who was who and what Carbonia was doing building an air base down in Xamon in the first place; and far as I could figure from Mike's talkings, it went something like this: Xamon was a small country, but thick with forests, and those forests were thick with really good quality wood, old, strong, hard wood, the kind people like to make elegant things out of, and along about thirty years ago this here corporation out of Carbonia called SangreDenar made itself a deal with the government of Xamon to harvest up those forests, to chop out as much wood as it could get its hands on and sell it to other companies for their manufacturing purposes; that went fine until ten or so years ago, when the forests started to shrink down a lot from all this harvesting, and then SangreDenar had to push deeper and deeper into the forests to keep getting wood. Now that would have been good and fine too, leastways as far as SangreDenar and the government of Xamon were concerned, but see, there were other people living deep in the forests, what Mike called "indigenous people" from a tribe called the Saridita, and way Mike told it, those people needed the forests to live, to keep doing things the way they and their ancestors had been doing them for generations.

So for a long while the Saridita and the government of Xamon took to negotiating and trying to work something out, with the government offering to move the Saridita out of the forests and into other parts of Xamon, and with the Saridita saying thanks but no thanks, they just wanted to keep living like they always had, well and with SangreDenar all the time saying that was all good and fine, but it just wanted its wood, which the government had said it could have, and which, if things didn't get fixed, SangreDenar would have to sue the government about, either in the courts of Xamon or in some other world-type court or

6

something. And along about that time SangreDenar started putting pressure on the government of Carbonia to build an air base down there, so that Carbonia could protect its "interests," as Mike said SangreDenar liked to put it, so about five years ago, which was about the time me and Mike had first taken to thinking of starting up a band together, Carbonia had built the air base and had kept fighter jets and helicopter gunships there ever since. Yeah, and about two years ago, some of the more radical of the Saridita, feeling frustrated by the talks with the government and how they thought the government was more worried about taking care of SangreDenar than about taking care of its own people, took to forming up an armed resistance, and the armed resistance eventually formed into the rebel army.

So these rebels, they took to attacking Xamon Army troops, either in convoys or at remote outposts, though they hadn't ever attacked in any of the cities, or tried to hit our air base or anything like that. Well and they hadn't ever attacked any SangreDenar people directly either, leastways not yet, though they had been known to sabotage SangreDenar equipment, stuff like bulldozers and other logging machinery, when there wasn't anybody using them and there weren't any guards around. So SangreDenar, they took to posting armed guards all over the place, and too they took to pressuring the government of Xamon to do something, so the government decided it was gonna put a stop to this rebel army, and it started an offensive against the rebels out in the forests. But you see, the Xamon Army, well, they aren't real bold and effective, as one might put it, being mostly made up of young kids that have been rounded up and drafted out of the slums of Xamon City, and being poorly trained and not paid right or regular, and not well equipped either; yeah, we'd seen the Xamon Army up close, even giving them some formal training on how to do night patrols and the like, being as how it seemed like any time they tried to go out at night they got hammered by the rebels, and being as how the rebels mostly operated at night and there wasn't any way the Xamon Army was gonna stop the rebels if they couldn't meet them out at night.

So meantime SangreDenar, they were getting pretty impatient with how the government and the Xamon Army were handling things, and too they were finding out that their armed guards weren't much better at dealing with the rebels than the Xamon Army was, being as how their guards all tended to fade into the background any time a lot of rebels were said to be around, which of course led to more sabotaging of SangreDenar's equipment, which of course was costing them money. And this is where things get kind of controversial, leastways according to Mike, because it was around that time, along about three or four months before me and Mike got to Xamon, that Mike says the paramilitaries started to operate; these paramilitaries, they were basically what you would call a private army, private soldiers that didn't officially exist and didn't officially have anything to do with the government of Xamon, and they were most shady and mysterious-like, usually moving in small groups of three or four people, and most always wearing solid black fatigues with no markings or insignia, and carrying brand new automatic weapons and grenades; and to hear Mike tell it, nobody was really sure who these paramilitaries worked for or what they were up to, but Mike had heard talk that they were getting paid by SangreDenar, or maybe through some kind of a joint arrangement between SangreDenar and the government of Xamon, and they were said to be real vicious-like and violent in the ways they went after the rebels.

And there was talk, including among our intelligence folks who were briefing us, that these paramilitaries weren't just after the rebels, but that they were doing things to any Saridita they came across, including Saridita who didn't have anything to do with the rebels and who supported talking more with the government of Xamon: like these paramilitaries were a lot more

9

interested in scaring and intimidating all the Saridita than they were in helping to put down the armed resistance of the few Saridita who'd become rebels. But far as we knew that was just talk, leastways we hadn't seen any evidence of it, though it did lead to one more complication, one more group of people running around out there in the forests of Xamon, and that was the human rights activists who were out there investigating all this talk about the paramilitaries and the rebels and the fighting in general, investigating and taking notes and otherwise trying to document everything that was going on, either for themselves, or for the press, or in case some day some kind of international tribunal or some such thing took to looking into it all; Mike said nobody was really sure how many human rights people were out there, nobody had an accurate count of how many organizations there even were, but far as he could figure from our briefings and such, they came from a variety of backgrounds, some being college students from Xamon City, others being your social worker types, others being other types of aid workers. Sometimes we'd get more explicit-like briefings about these people, when more was known, including pictures of them so we'd know them if we saw them and we could stay away from them.

Which kind of leads to where we fit in to the whole big mess, which to me was sometimes the most confusing part of it all. See, according to Mike, about the same time SangreDenar took to forming up these paramilitary squads--if in fact they were the ones behind the squads--SangreDenar also took to putting pressure on the government of Carbonia to get more involved, to send in troops to help SangreDenar out of its little jam; and turns out that was a pretty touchy subject, being as how Carbonia had so much else going on with the wars in Shiraz and Anaiza raging away full strength and occupying such a big part of the Carbonia Army, and even leading people to be talking about a draft and such, that the government couldn't really spare any more infantry troops or special forces. So what they did instead, to appease SangreDenar, as Mike had heard it said, was to send in more Air Corps security forces troops, under the guise of guarding the air base, but really to work as bodyguards for SangreDenar bigwigs and to gather information for the Carbonia government and whoever it might want to share that information with.

Leastways that's how Mike explained it all to me, near as I can remember now; might be a little simple, and maybe a little fuzzy on some of the details, being as how politics isn't really my thing, like I mentioned

11

earlier, but it gives the main ideas anyway, and kind of explains how Carbonia got all tangled up in things down in Xamon. Now as for how me and Mike got drawn into it all and ended up on a path in the forest waiting to get shot at, that's a little easier, being as how I was there firsthand, being as how I remember it all pretty fresh and solid. We'd talked about joining up before, with Mike talking about us getting in ahead of the draft, and getting out of Nyala and all, but we hadn't really decided anything for sure, it more just being talk and all. But see, then there came along this big songwriting contest, sponsored by one of the top radio stations in Nyala, and of course Mike and me had to try to win. Problem being, we didn't have any sort of band together, no drummer or bass player, just me on the guitar and Mike on the vocals, and no finished songs either, leastways not anything with both words and music all done up and finished. Me, I'd written quite a few instrumentals, and Mike, he'd written a notebook full of lyrics; it was putting it all together into a good song that we were lacking in, and not because we hadn't been trying. No, we'd spent quite a bit of time together working on it, and we had some stuff that was pretty close to done, but nothing that the two of us were totally happy about, well or leastways nothing Mike was totally happy about, because truth be told I never was quite as picky as Mike was, and I thought some of our stuff was pretty good, if I do mention it myself. But still, we didn't have a band, which would have wrinkled things up even if we had had songs.

Of course Mike, he was never the sort to get stopped in his tracks by something like that, and he sure as shooting wasn't about to let this songwriting contest get by us, so he studied it a bit, and by and by he said he figured we'd have to come up with an acoustic song, just guitar and vocals, and then get it recorded up as best we could and turn it in for the contest. And he wanted it to be something nice and slow and melodic, even though mostly we wrote faster stuff, songs with what you might call a harder edge. Me, I could see his point, being as how on the radio they're always wanting nice slow melodic-type songs, the sort people can hum or sing along with, the kind they can nod their heads and sway to; so me, I took to going over some ideas I'd been working up, and I settled on a slow, soft tune I'd been working on for the last month or so; it was a sad, melancholy thing, sort of gloomy and hollow, like a body might want to hear on a gray stormy afternoon full of clouds and drizzle and unhappy people, and first time I played it for Mike, he nodded deep and crinkled up his eyebrows, then he made that little clicking sound out of the corner of his mouth.

"Yeah, Eddie-man," he said, still nodding, half with a smile, half with a scowl, "that's exactly what we need, that's exactly what will get us played on the radio." And then he took to pacing a bit, looking all perplexed-like and serious, like he was thinking real hard; and of course I knew from experience that meant he was trying to figure up some lyrics, some kind of "hook" as he liked to call it that people would like and remember and that would make our song a hit. Now we didn't have a whole lot of time, being as how the contest deadline was only about two weeks away, but the next day he came back to me with an idea for a title, sort of a "concept," as he called it; his idea was to call the song "Something More," and he said how he was gonna write up some words about looking for something more in life, something more than what you're born with, and the town you live in, and the chances you have for living a good life there; and that sounded good to me, that sounded like a fine and fitting idea for such a quiet and tender-like tune, and too it sounded like it summed up and fit our lives just about perfect, what we were looking for, what we were hoping for; so I waited and waited, but Mike didn't ever come to me with anything. Every day we talked about it, and every day Mike said he was working on it, but more and more he seemed to just get frustrated, so that his mood was just plain vile and black, so that not even I could hardly tolerate being around him; and try as I might, kind of gently-like prodding him, he wouldn't show me any of the lyrics he'd been working on.

"Not until they're all done, not until I'm totally satisfied with them," he would say, shaking his head, scowling and kind of sucking his top lip down into his mouth, kind of pinching it there and gripping it with his teeth; and me, I knew Mike well enough to just let it lie, and to hope that he'd come up with something in time for us to get it recorded and turned in, and I knew too that Mike didn't need any reminding of when the deadline was, that if there was anyone in Nyala who had heard about the contest and knew for sure when the deadline was, it would be Mike. But as time got closer he just got more and more black and vile, so that really I was most dreading seeing him, all up until the day before the deadline, and then it was like it had all blown over and gone away, and Mike seemed all calm and serene-like, all patient and reserved and determined. And that's when he told me it was time for us to join the Air Corps.

"We've talked about it and talked about it," he started, standing with his hands on his hips, kind of cocking his head at an angle and nodding a bit. "Now,

15

Eddie-man, we just need to do it. We just need to take a stand for ourselves and do it. Two years is all it is, Eddie-man, two short years. By then we'll know if the draft is coming, and we can stay in longer if we have to."

Well and me, I wasn't so sure, because even though I kind of agreed with Mike about Nyala and us needing to get out of there and such, I wasn't so set about the Air Corps, about how we'd do in there and fit in and all; but Mike, he'd always looked out for me before, if anybody had ever tried to pick on me or anything, being as how Mike, he was stocky and all-over muscular, whereas me, I was more of the tall and lean sort, maybe even what you might call slight; and he'd always told me that he'd look out for me in the Air Corps too, and that I wouldn't have to worry about anything as long as we joined up together. So that same day we went down and talked to a recruiter, and he set to work trying to sell us big on going into the security forces, saying that's where all the fun and excitement was; and Mike, he seemed to go along with that, seemed to be taking it all in and sorting it out, so me, I just went along too.

And it isn't like we got shipped straight to Xamon, but it was pretty close, truth be told. First of course we had to go to basic training, and then to the security forces tech school, and all told that took us nearways five months, what with six weeks for basic training and another 14 weeks for our tech school. Me, I wasn't too crazy about basic training, being as how it seemed like it was all just a bunch of yelling and screaming and anger over nothing, far as I was concerned. Truth be told, it started out pretty rough for me, because even though I like to think of myself as not a downright stupid kind of person, it was pretty intimidating with all those drill instructors coming up and barking out orders and such, and me, I just couldn't seem to get the hang of things, of how to march in time with everyone else, or of how to fold my shirts and socks in just the exact particular way the drill instructors wanted everything folded; and Mike, he helped me all he could, even doing most of my folding for me, when it was lights out time and all the drill instructors had gone home for the day, and helping me learn to shine up my combat boots, and even trying to give me tips on my marching and my saluting and other such things.

But I just couldn't seem to get things, and seemed to me the drill instructors were out to make me most miserable about it, so things stayed pretty rough, leastways up until halfway through the fourth week of training, when we went out to learn to shoot the M16. Now me, I'd never shot any kind of gun before, let

17

alone an automatic rifle, and truth be told I didn't take much stock in the chances of me doing very well either; no, seemed to me there was as good a chance I'd end up shooting myself as there was I'd end up hitting my target even once. But somehow it didn't turn out that way; rather, that M16 just felt kind of loose and comfortable in my arms, almost the way my guitar felt, and even though I wouldn't say I enjoyed shooting, or really cared much to do it again, my shots all took to going where I aimed them, and even though none of the combat arms instructors out there could seem to believe it, I fired a near perfect score on all the exercises, from standing, and kneeling, and lying down flat, and too from out in the open, and behind a barricade, and to the side of the barricade; and those instructors just looked at my target and shook their heads, counting and recounting the bullet holes in the cardboard silhouette, I guess just to make sure that what they were seeing was the truth of the thing; and finally they said it was, and that I'd shot what the Carbonia Air Corps called "Expert," which would qualify me for a special ribbon on my dress uniform. Which sounded nice enough, though I really didn't know when or why I'd ever be wearing my dress uniform.

When we got back to the barracks and the drill

instructors got our scores, none of them could believe it either, and they looked those scores over a few times, well and then talked quietly amongst themselves, and from then on they called me "Sharpshooter," which believe me was a lot better than some of the things they'd been calling me before. Now Mike, he still called me Eddie-man, just like he always had, but you could tell he was excited about it too, and that evening after all the drill instructors were gone and we had a few minutes before lights out, he smiled and patted me on the back, and then he nudged me kind of playfully with his elbow and made that little clicking sound of his, and told me my good shooting was probably on account of all my guitar playing, of all the hand and eye coordination I'd developed over the years. And me, I didn't know if there was any truth to that or not, but seemed like it was as good an explanation as anything else, so I nodded and agreed with him.

"Just wait, Eddie-man," he added, nodding in that knowing way of his, "they're gonna start treating you a lot better after this. You've got a gift, Eddie, and now they can finally see that."

And come to find he was right, though I never would have predicted it: the drill instructors did start treating me better, and they didn't seem to ride my case so hard about my folding and my saluting and my marching, all of which, sad to say, were still most terrible. Two days after the shooting range we went out to the base annex, which was a big outdoors campsite with makeshift tents and bunkers all made up to be like a real deployment somewhere; and out there we had what was called our FTX, or Field Training Exercise, and that went pretty well for me too. Basically it was like a big night-long war game, with us basic trainees being told we had to defend the camp all through the night while the same combat arms training instructors who had taught us the M16 earlier in the week took the role of attacking us; and see, they had real M16s modified to shoot laser lights instead of bullets, so they could tell when they knocked us off; yeah and we just had our little flashlights with cones on top of them--the same flashlights we used when we marched off to Physical Training in the dark every morning--to try to shoot back with.

Well so me and Mike, we got assigned to a bunker out on the perimeter of the camp, right near the woods, and we dug in best we could and peered out there into the treelines, which were pretty dark and spooky-looking, being as how there wasn't but a sliver of a moon that night, well and being as how the whole place was kind of faraway and foreign to us anyhow, not being from anywhere around those parts; and it wasn't long before we started seeing those little red laser lights from their rifles come scooting along the trail right outside our bunker, coming straight from a thick clump of trees directly in front of the bunker, nearways thirty-five or forty yards away; and we just kept low and watched out best we could, wondering how many of them were out there, wondering too if they'd try to overrun us or just sniper us off; so me, I edged out the far side of the bunker, the side away from the trail, being as how out that way there was another line of trees, one we weren't getting any fire from.

So I worked myself out there best I could, flat on my belly, just barely crawling along, figuring that at any minute they'd shift their laser shots my way and I'd be a goner; but they didn't, but rather they just kept firing those little skip shots right down the trail, so me, I crawled out even farther and then turned and angled myself back to the direction they were firing from, and then I lit up my flashlight at them all rapid-fire style, flicking it on and off, to simulate automatic rifle fire, just the way we'd been told to do; and far as I could figure I hit at least one of them square on, judging from where my light was aimed and where the laser shots were coming from, and all quick-like they stopped their firing, but they didn't any of them go down or otherwise acknowledge being shot. And I guess that's just the way things go in a situation like that: if it had been one of us who'd been shot they'd have made sure we knew about it, but being as how it was one of them they weren't gonna say anything. Which was all the same to me, being as how it was just pretend and all.

So me, I scurried on back into the bunker after that, figuring it wouldn't be long before they repositioned themselves and took to firing on us again; and I was right, only now there were at least two of them trying to pick us off, one firing along the trail side of the bunker, the other firing along the far side, and then both of them closing in on us a bit; so me and Mike, we just sunk down into that bunker low as we could, not daring to move, watching the laser shots play all over the sandbags surrounding us. That went on for ten or so minutes, then it dropped off all abrupt-like, and we didn't know if they figured they'd got us or if they were just repositioning to try to soften up the camp from another angle. We kept to waiting, leastways twenty-five or thirty minutes, and far as I was concerned we could just sit there and wait all night, being as how we didn't have anything else to do; but Mike, he was getting kind of antsy and impatient, so he leaned over close to me and whispered that he was gonna peek his head around the side of the bunker--the side closest to the trail, not the side I'd crawled out of earlier--and see if there was any movement out there.

Now me, I didn't like that idea at all, being as how these combat arms instructors had briefed us earlier about the importance of being patient in a tight situation, the importance of not doing anything too hasty-like, and being as how I figured that meant they were aiming to teach us something about patience that night during our FTX; so me, I tried to tell Mike that, but he wasn't much for listening just then; rather, he shook his head at me and kind of scowled, then whispered something about what if they were about to overrun our position, and I didn't really have any answer to that, other than that maybe we should have brought us out a little mirror or something we could have rigged up to see out the bunker with, and he just shrugged and said something about that not helping us now, and then he kind of pivoted his body around and took to inching near the edge of the bunker. And me, I took to bracing myself up over in my corner of the bunker, with a bad feeling in my stomach that we were about to see a load more laser shots.

Mike, he inched closer and closer, and it was so quiet and tense-like I could hear every breath he took and every little sigh-like noise he made as he scooted out on his belly and chest, and then I heard him swallow hard, and real quick-like he popped his head

23

past the edge of the sandbags, raising up on his toes just a pinch as he did so; and all instant-like the red laser lights started up again, and out of nowhere they were all of sudden bouncing along the side of Mike's head, dotting his ear, and his cheek, and even up along his forehead.

"Ah, man," Mike groaned, kind of scowling and shaking his head ever so slightly, then rolling along on the bridge of his neck, so that his eyes and face were up to the sky, and then following that through with his shoulders, so that his whole body was face up, looking like a new-dead corpse, like he had just fallen from the sky or something. "Chalk one up for the Eddie-man," he muttered, "you sure called that one." Then he just laid there playing dead, just like we'd been told to do if we got hit, and me, I stayed down flat as I could, watching the laser shots as they kept pinging about on the sandbags, probing for a good shot on me. And not long after that they got on the loudspeakers--which in military talk they called the "giant voice" system--and announced the end of the first round, and that all the "casualties" had to report to the main tent area for a debriefing, and that the rest of us could take a five minute break and get repositioned. So Mike, he hauled himself up and trotted off to the tent area, patting my back and calling out a quick "Good luck, Eddie-man" on his way.

And me, I was kind of sad and lonely-like to see him go, but I knew too that I didn't have but five minutes before the exercise would start up again, so I real quick-like scampered up out of the bunker and slid over into the shadow of the nearest tree, maybe ten or twelve feet out the far side of the bunker, and I hugged myself all close up against that tree and hunkered down for round two; see, I figured I hadn't seen the end of those laser shots, and I figured too there wasn't any way I was gonna be anything but pinned down if I stayed in that bunker, and that if I wasn't careful the firing this time wouldn't be coming from right in front of the bunker, but maybe from the trees off here to the side, which would put me in a most miserable position if I was still perched there in the bunker, nothing more than a speed bump waiting to get run over. And me, I knew a thing or two about patience myself, you know, with living in Nyala, and waiting on Mike to write up some just perfect lyrics for "Something More," and just living my life in general; so I figured I could wait out these here combat arms training instructors, if that's what the situation required of me, and that's exactly what I aimed to do.

Our five minute break up and ended about the time I got good and settled, and then I really perked up and took to listening and watching and observing things with all my senses; and too I got to noticing the night, really noticing it, like the sweet pine-like smell in the air, and the quiet, ghost-like breeze playing in the trees, kind of prickling and chilling me, making me feel kinda anxious and nervous-like, but also making me feel all vibrant-like and happy and glad to be alive; but mostly I kept my eyes focused on that far-off line of trees right smack in front of the bunker, where the instructors had been firing from before, being as how I figured they'd start somewhere out there, no matter where they intended to eventually go. So I waited and waited, way more than an hour, probably even two, never moving from my spot, part of my mind staying all keen and sharp on what was going on around me, another part taking to thinking about my guitar, which was back home, and different songs I'd learned from the radio or from CDs, and different chords and riffs I'd written all on my own. And even though I was beginning to feel a little better about the Air Corps, after shooting so well with the M16 and all, still I was a little nervous, a little antsy, and truth be told a part of me was wondering if we'd done the right thing by joining up, or if maybe we'd have done better just to stay in Nyala and keep focusing on our music there. Mike had never steered me wrong before, and I didn't want to think that maybe

26

he had now, but really I couldn't tell, really I couldn't tell at all.

Finally I took to seeing some kind of movement about twenty feet in front of our old bunker, and though I didn't dare to move myself, or hardly even to draw in a single breath, still I squinted up my eyes and tried hard to focus, and far as I could figure there was someone sprawled out all flat-like and crawling, ever so slowly, in the direction of the bunker; and scanning real close-like around where that first person was, seemed to me there might be another figure about ten feet back and six feet to the left of the first one, but truly I couldn't be for sure; and of course seeing that took my mind to all-over conjuring and imagining, and after that it seemed like I was seeing crawling figures everywhere, and between that and the tickling, ghost-like breeze I took to feeling most all-over spooked and jolted, and frankly I wasn't sure what to do or where to go. Still, far as I could figure nobody had spotted me yet, leastways nobody had gotten a mind to shoot at me, and that helped to calm me down a bit, helped me to breathe deep and slow and study up what to do. And seemed to me the best thing to do was just to keep watching, just to see how many people there were attacking, and too to let whoever it was get good and close so that when I opened up on them they wouldn't be able to pretend they weren't hit. So I took to letting my patience have sway again, and I just breathed regular as I could and stood still as I could, taking in the evening, imagining I was just out for a midnight ambling and had stopped to watch an alley cat, or an owl, or some other night-type creature.

Took a couple of minutes, but finally I was sure there were only two of them, moving only a little at a time, one moving first, then the other; yeah, and now I was sure too from the markings of their uniforms that they were both instructors, and I could just catch a glint of metal every now and again from the barrels of their M16s. And me, I'd already decided that unless they saw me first and I had to fire to keep from them getting me, I wasn't gonna open up or so much as move at all until they were right up on the bunker, maybe even until they'd peeked in there and seen that it was empty. But the closer they got the harder it was, me feeling kind of antsy and nervous, like maybe they'd change their minds and start to crawling back yonder to the treeline, or maybe they'd see me but I wouldn't know it, and then I'd lose my advantage and get taken down myself, which did seem like a powerful shame after so much patience and waiting on my part; so when they got about five feet from the edge of the bunker I spun down to a knee and lit up on them, flicking my flashlight on and off to beat the devil, tagging first one and then the other with my beam, feeling a strange calmness and collectedness sweep over me. And for a second I wasn't sure they were gonna admit to being shot even then, even dead as a doornail could be, and truth be told from the looks on their faces I was afraid I might have just walked myself into a heap load of trouble, being as how they didn't look any bit too happy to get ambushed that way, especially not by a basic trainee, and a tall, lean, slight one at that; well but after three or four seconds of me staring at them and them staring at me, and a little bit of foul language on their part, if I do say, they both got up off the ground and took to shaking their heads, looking at each other, then over at me, then at each other again; and finally one of them said "Nice job, airman," though he said it almost like an afterthought, and he didn't really look me square in the eye or anything when he spoke it.

And again when we got back to the basic training barracks and the drill instructors took to seeing our FTX evaluations, they just shook their heads, and talked quietly amongst themselves for a bit, and the rest of basic training was smooth sailing for me, and I didn't fail any more of my inspections or anything; which seemed kind of strange, truth be told, and almost a little unfair, being as how I still couldn't fold my shirts and socks and underwear quite right, well and certainly I couldn't get them all ironed down and flat like they were supposed to be; nor shine my boots worth a bit, nor salute, nor take to remembering most of the Carbonia Air Corps history they taught us in the classroom sessions. And tech school was just the same, though I did feel like it was more fair and less biased-like, being as how in tech school we didn't have long classroom sessions about history, and we didn't have inspections to see if we'd ironed and folded our clothes just right; rather, we spent all our time on more substantial things, practical things, like training on all the weapons systems we had to get proficient on, and learning basic air base security strategies, and patrol tactics and ambushing and something called LPOP, which was military shorthand for "listening post, observation post." The instructors at the tech school, they told me and Mike they were gonna train us two up special on the LPOP stuff, based on my shooting scores and what they called my "stealth skills" at the FTX, and based on Mike's overall learning scores, which were always higher than mine by a long shot.

And the way LPOP worked was that a team of people, usually two, but sometimes four, depending on the mission requirements, and how hostile the environment was, and how big or small of a "footprint" one wanted to leave, would take to monitoring a certain location, like a trail, or a highway, or a bridge, or maybe a suspected safe house, or an enemy base, to find out exactly what was going on out there in a real live situational way, in a way a video camera, or a sensor, or any other electronic intelligence gathering machine we had in Carbonia couldn't do; and the idea behind it being a listening post and observation post was that the team wasn't ever supposed to engage the enemy, though the teams were always armed, just in case, and too the teams weren't ever supposed to let on that they were there; and how that worked was that you'd usually scout out your location, and consider the geography of it in terms of what your mission or objective was, and then pick out the ideal spot for the team to bed down and conceal itself and take to observing and gathering information. And if it was a two-person team, which is what we most trained up for, being as how the instructors told us that was what we were most likely to use out in field situations, the two would find their spot and then lie down flat, facing away from each other, so between them they could cover the full 360 degrees around them, with their feet either barely touching or being just close enough to touch, so that they could signal one another when something started to happen; and there was a whole mess of signals they taught us how to use, but I won't go into all that just now, being as how it could get a bit confusing, and being as how I wasn't always that great at remembering some of the more complicated-type signals and such anyhow.

The main point of it was to stay concealed and secret, no matter how close anyone got to you, so we trained up a lot on that, on the discipline, you might say, of staying put and staying concealed even when you thought you were about to be found out; and the instructors, they told lots of stories and legends of course, like how an enemy soldier ought to be able to come up and relieve himself right on your location without ever knowing you're there, and other such stories like that, and we just mostly took it all in and absorbed it best we could, hoping we wouldn't ever encounter any situations like that.

Too there was a variation on LPOP that we trained up on, what the Air Corps called a Recon Patrol, which was military shorthand for reconnaissance patrol, and was kind of like a perimeter patrol and an LPOP rolled into one; the way it worked was they'd break us into teams of two, just like LPOP teams, and they'd send us out to scour a certain area, much bigger than anything we'd do on a perimeter patrol, and much more broad and unfocused than any kind of specific LPOP mission,

32

but with some elements of both just the same: elements of a perimeter patrol in that we were on foot and spent most of the time on the patrols moving around, not stationary like LPOPs, being as how we had a certain area to cover, and usually a fairly large one at that; but elements of LPOP too, in that we had to be all stealthy and quiet and as concealed as possible, and also in that sometimes if we came across something odd or out of place-like we'd take to bedding down and observing it for a piece; and too like LPOP because we had strict orders not to engage anyone except in self-defense, but rather only to gather information and report back to the base with it.

Then tech school finished up, and me and Mike got orders to Xamon, and before we knew it we were out there doing all those tech school things for real, like small team patrols around the perimeter of the air base, and LPOP a little farther out, and even Recon Patrols out deep in the forest. We had to be kind of careful when we ventured too far out from the base and into the woods, being as how that was kind of sensitive, being as how we weren't really supposed to be doing that and the government of Xamon might take that as us spying on them and such; so when we went out there we had to be extra careful to hide ourselves most slick and thorough, and to hide our tracks too, so that when we left nobody would have any clues we'd been there.

It was a Recon Patrol we were on that morning, making our way down a thin little forager's trail we'd stumbled across along about four miles out from the air base; and funny thing was the whole morning had been all still and quiet and peaceful-like up until that sharp, whacking sound had come: me and Mike, we'd woken up in fine and pleasant and joking moods, and truth be told those type moods were getting more and more rare, because there was such a shortage of security forces troops with the other wars going on and all that we worked pretty much all the time, usually twelve hours on and twelve hours off, which after a while starts to take a toll on a body; but still those fine, pleasant moods came, time to time leastways, and we had one that morning, being all jovial and content-like, feeling that maybe life really was mighty free and easy after all, being as how we'd pulled a Recon Patrol and not a perimeter patrol or guard post duty, both of which were most dreadful and boring, and too being as how we were looking at a couple of days out from the air base, if we could conjure up a reason to be out that long.

See, with these Recon Patrols they were giving us a whole lot more freedom and space to decide for ourselves about how long to stay out, so that now instead of only going out for a few hours and having strict orders on the latest time we could report back in, like we did on LPOP, we now could stay out overnight--up to a maximum of 36 hours--if we came across something hot that needed close watching. And troop shortage or no troop shortage, that seemed like a lot of responsibility, a lot of autonomy, as Mike liked to say, to be placing on a couple of two-stripers, which is what we were; but me and Mike, we figured there were leastways some good things about being out on patrol, because even though we'd both been born and raised in Nyala, which was mostly city, and hadn't really spent any time in woods as thick and sprawling as the woods in Xamon, we both were taking to liking the woods, and we both were getting pretty good at handling ourselves and navigating around out there too. And truth be told, we hadn't run into anything much on any of our earlier patrols, them mostly just being routine, and really we weren't expecting to run into anything that morning either; sure, we'd caught far off glimpses of Xamon Army regulars on patrol, or had stumbled across their cigarette butts--well because those Xamon Army regulars couldn't cover their tracks worth a lick--but we hadn't seen any rebels, or any paramilitaries, or anyone else but the occasional villager out foraging up some food. So most always when we drew a Recon Patrol we'd stay out as long as we could, well and Mike would always come up with a good cover story to explain why we'd found it necessary to be gone so long, his story usually involving us thinking we were on to something, well and tracking it a bit, well and then discovering it really wasn't anything after all. Which maybe made us seem a little silly, but kept us out of trouble anyway.

But Mike, he was getting to be a little unsure about these Recon Patrols, because even though we hadn't run into any action yet, and didn't generally have much information to report back with--leastways much information that seemed important to us--he said he saw some ominous and frightful-like signs about the way things were going lately: for one, he was suspicious of what was happening to whatever information we did bring back, whether it was just going to our own Air Corps intelligence folks, for better base security, well or if, as he was starting to suspect, it was getting sent up the channel to other parts of the Carbonia government, and maybe from there to SangreDenar, and maybe from there back to the paramilitaries. And even though Mike didn't have any evidence to support him, he said it seemed to him like if that was what was happening, well we were being had, we were being used for something we hadn't signed ourselves up for. No, Mike would stop and ponder on it, and he'd always say how he couldn't see at all how gathering information that was just gonna get fed down to some big fancy corporation like SangreDenar, and maybe even to some outlaw private army like those there paramilitaries, pertained to our mission, how it connected with serving and protecting the citizens of Carbonia, which is what they'd taught us in basic training the Carbonia Air Corps was supposed to be all about. So Mike, he kept saying how he was gonna set up a little experiment to see if he could figure out where our information was going, that he was gonna come up with a real tantalizing cover story and see where it ended up, but so far he hadn't done that, which was just fine with me, since far as I could figure going out on a limb like that was just asking for trouble.

But another thing bothered Mike too, and it was beginning to eat away at me as well: we'd been told we had to wear "sanitized" uniforms any time we did LPOP or Recon Patrols, which meant we wore the same old camouflage uniforms and flak vests and web belts as usual, only now nothing could have our name or rank anywhere on it, nor could it in any way identify with the Carbonia Air Corps, which meant we had to go so far as to strip the little manufacturer's labels off our clothing and all our gear. Now me, I couldn't figure out why they'd want us to do that, but Mike, he just scowled and said maybe it was for "plausible deniability," which meant that if we got caught out where we weren't supposed to be--which when it came to the woods was pretty much everywhere outside the perimeter of the air base--then our own government could deny we were there on their authority, or even with their knowledge. To me that seemed pretty low down and dirty, even if some of the other things Mike had heard about the government of Carbonia and its relationship with SangreDenar were true, but like I said earlier, Mike, he was pretty sharp, and I took stock in most everything he said when it came to thinking things out, so as much as I didn't want to believe my own government could do such a thing to the airmen out there trying to protect it, I was getting me some hesitations about these Recon Patrols myself.

And one other thing: we weren't allowed to carry LMRs--which were land mobile radios, in military talk, or what you might call walkie-talkies--with us anymore; and the reason we were given was that the LMRs didn't have the range for these longer patrols, which was true enough, but as Mike said that didn't mean they couldn't give us some other type of radio or equipment in case we got in a jam and needed help or an extraction or even some kind of air strike or covering fire; but the way they answered that--because Mike, he even brought it up at a roll call--was to say that it was our job not to get into jams, that's what the Air Corps was paying us for, and other such talk as that, which needless to say didn't sit too well with Mike, or with me for that matter.

So good moods or not, still it was with a bit of uneasiness and hesitation that we mustered up that morning to get our daily patrol briefing, which included assigning the "sector" as they put it that we were to patrol, as well as the regular daily intelligence briefing, and also any specific information we might need about what was thought or known to be happening in that sector. As for that last part, when the intelligence officer who was briefing us got to the sector me and Mike had, he passed us out three little sheets of paper, each about six inches by nine inches, all laminated up to be waterproof, and punched with little spiral holes at the top, so that they could fit into the patrol notebooks we carried. All in all the notebooks were pretty handy, if I do say; they had maps of each sector we patrolled, and also maps of Xamon as a whole, and even a "bird's eye view" map showing Xamon and all the countries that surrounded it; and too they had information about call signs and certain code words used by the Xamon

Army, and the rebels as well, which would have been helpful if we still had LMRs, but now kind of just took up space and fattened up the notebooks for no reason; and of course all the information was just laid out all plain and nondescript, without any reference at all to Carbonia, which Mike figured was so that if it got found a body couldn't be all the way sure who had fixed it up and put it all together; more "plausible deniability," he liked to say. Too there were blank sheets in the notebooks, for us to take notes or make diagrams or do whatever else we needed to do to remember anything significant that we saw, though seemed like the intelligence officers were always encouraging us not to write down any more than we had to, and we couldn't help but wonder if that too was in case we got found out.

The new pages, the three we got that morning, they were fact sheets about three human rights workers who were rumored to be in the area, gathering up their own information about what was going on and who was doing what to who; "non-helpful noncombatants," that's what the Defense Minister of Carbonia called them, and as I said earlier we had strict orders to stay away from them, being as how we didn't want to be seen so far out in the field and all. The fact sheets gave what background information was known about each of them, and had a picture of each one also, so we took a few minutes to look them over and study them up, and Mike, he flipped through his faster than I flipped through mine, and when he got to the third one, he kind of nudged me and half smiled, and then winked and made his clicking sound.

"She's kind of cute," he whispered, tapping the third picture with his index finger, angling his notebook a little closer to me, like maybe I didn't have my own; and me, I was glad to see Mike being so all-over happy and gleeful, especially since things had been so glum lately, but too I was afraid his talking and stirring around was gonna call attention to us, was gonna get the intelligence folks up on us, and see, they weren't exactly known for their senses of humor or playfulness; so me, I just nodded real quick-like and took to flipping to the third page myself, hoping Mike would settle down a bit, leastways until after we got away from the briefing and out into the field. And when I got to the third page I didn't look straight at the picture, but instead I started with the reading part, being as how that's how I always liked to do things, since sometimes it took me a little longer than some people to read things, well and being as how I didn't want to miss anything important, you see; so me, I scanned through the name and background information, and come to find that this here human rights worker was named Digna Giraldo Cardona, and that she was thought to be nineteen or twenty years old, and that she'd spent a year at Xamon University before getting expelled for "activist activities" like speaking out on behalf of the Saridita, and against the government of Xamon, and SangreDenar, and even the government of Carbonia. And too it gave her approximate height and weight, and her hair and eye color and other such statistics, and told how she was fluent in our language--which most folks from Xamon City, leastways most educated folks, were--but really there wasn't much else of substance known about her, leastways not much our intelligence folks thought we needed to know.

So then I took to studying up her picture, which seemed to be an action shot of her marching along at some kind of political rally or other such gathering; and looked like it was taken by some kind of government agent or spy, because there wasn't any posing about it, no smiling for the camera, and it didn't seem close-up enough to have been taken by a news photographer or anyone like that; and truth be told, Mike was right, she was rather fetching, in her own way: she was a small woman, right at five feet if our sheet was to be believed, and thin as a rail, her weight being guessed at ninety-five to a hundred pounds; and in the picture she looked mighty thin too, almost thin as a child, and frankly not so healthy-like; more worried-down-to-the-bone thin, as one might say; but she had a spark to her, in her eyes, in the angle of her body as she strode along--kind of tilting forward, you might say--that seemed fierce and full of passion and vigor; and too she had long black hair, and dark brown or black eyes, and rich dark skin; but mostly it was her eyes, well because they seemed to speak of something faraway and beautiful, something most people couldn't see or know. Leastways seemed that way to me, for whatever that's worth. And me, I took next to studying up the other two pages, to find out as much as I could about these other two human rights workers; they were both men, one about thirty-five, the other about forty-five, and apparently all three were thought to be traveling together, and were thought to be working for the same human rights group. I checked to see if there was any other information on them, maybe on the back of the sheets, and when I was good and convinced I'd seen all there was to see, I slipped the pages into my notebook and put it away, then me and Mike took to gathering up our gear and heading out.

And truth be told we started out that morning all calm and happy and optimistic-like, almost like we were a couple of kids going camping, and we were all grins and smiles when we hopped up into the back of the three-quarter ton truck that drove us out to our drop point, and even as we took to walking our regular springing-off trail we were pretty carefree and jaunty. But see, even in a good mood, even kind of jubilant, we knew we had to keep our wits up, so as we moved farther off the perimeter of the base, as we dug deeper off into the sector we were moving into, we took to being more calm and sedate and attentive-like.

It didn't take us long to get into a pretty good groove, moving along cautiously but at a nice-paced clip, keeping our eyes peeled and our senses sharp; see, we hadn't ever patrolled this particular sector before, it being all alien-like and foreign to us, and it going right smack flush with the border of Tyumen, which was the country directly to the east of Xamon; we'd been briefed that the border wasn't very closely guarded, leastways not out here in the country, well but that things did get kind of hectic and heavy around about Zadar, which came close to straddling the border and which was the nearest Tyumen city of any size. All told we knew we had to be extra cautious, and had to plot out on our maps what kind of course would keep us out of too much hassle; so Mike, he planned us up a good route, one he figured was likely to be easy and quiet--because as you can imagine Mike had pretty much taken to looking for ways to get by with as little ruckus as possible and still get us far enough away from the base that we wouldn't get caught what they called "malingering"--and with all our misgivings about doing Recon Patrols, me, I was right with him on the matter of us finding an easy, quiet way to do our business and then get back home.

So we went along all peaceful and uneventful-like until about mid-morning, until we got about four miles from the base and found us that foraging trail and took to making our way down it; and then we were trapped, leastways it seemed so to us, as we gripped our rifles and stood stock still as we could, ready to dive for cover but scared to move, just in case whoever had made that whacking noise hadn't seen or heard us yet. Mike, he was out in front of me about ten feet, way he usually was when we walked single-file on a trail, so I could see his every move; and seemed like we stood there dead still forever, so that my knees took to wobbling a little, so that my ankles began to ache. Mike, he stood mostly still as well, though he did move a little, kind of shifting his weight from foot to foot, craning his head around ever so slightly and noiselessly, to see as much of the area ahead of us as he could; but we didn't either of us see or hear a thing, not for leastways two or three solid minutes, so finally

Mike, he twisted at his waist and looked back to me, and with just the slightest jerk of his head he motioned for me to move up to where he was. And me, I could see that his eyes were wide open and all alert-like, and that his mouth and the lines along it were drawn up all tight and solid--filled with tension, one might say-- which of course took to making me even more nervous than I already was, which truth be told was pretty nervous; so me, I real slow and cautious-like started to move toward him, my finger right up near the trigger of my rifle, but not so close on it that I might fire without meaning to. I was breathing kind of fast, and my palms were sweating and my fingers were even twitching a piece, and my heart was taking to pounding something fierce; but me, I just kept trying to calm myself, kept trying to tell myself to stay cool and keep my thoughts together best I could, being as how I figured that losing my head wouldn't help us any; but it was hard, real hard, because every step I took seemed like it rang through that forest like static on the giant voice, and every little odd noise that came about as I moved, like the leather of my combat boot creaking or the water in my canteen swishing around, seemed to me like it was howling louder than a shotgun blast, rattling off the nearby trees and echoing on down the trail.

Finally, though, I got up close to where Mike was,

maybe three feet from him, and Mike, he real slow-like lifted his back hand off his rifle and motioned me to hold up; and then he motioned to the left with his head, and then he took to working his way sideways in that direction; which I took to mean he wanted to get off the trail and take cover in the underbrush, leastways until we could be sure what was going on; so me, I waited until he was off the trail and crouched down in some bushes, and then I kind of sidewindered myself over there too. And we sat there stock still and waited a good twenty-five or thirty minutes, but we didn't see nor hear so much as a peep out of the ordinary. So Mike, he leaned over close to me and whispered all raspy-like to me.

"Let's keep going that way," he said, nodding in the direction we'd originally been heading. "We'll just stay in the woods instead of using the trail." And me, I nodded back, even though I knew that creeping through the woods without making noise would be no easy task, and that some of the underbrush around us was pretty thick and tangly, which too would slow us down quite a bit. Mike, he raised himself up and took to working his way deeper into the woods, so that he was parallel to the trail but a good fifteen feet to the left of it, and me, I worked my way over there too, stepping what you might call careful-like and gingerly; my nerves, they had worked themselves back down to normal, and truth be told I didn't think we'd come across anything, being as how I figured that whatever had made the noise was probably just an animal, and that by now it was probably long gone on its way. But still a part of me was curious, and I guess a part of Mike was too, being as how he wanted to keep on going rather than turn back; and odd as it may sound, I definitely had a sort of tingly feeling deep down in my stomach, like something was about to happen, something all strange and out of the ordinary.

So we kept to moving along, careful to be as quiet as we could, careful too to stay parallel with the original trail, but that wasn't always easy, being as how sometimes the underbrush got so thick we could hardly even see the trail, could hardly even make our way through it. After we'd tracked our way like that for another hour or so, Mike, he took to heading more to the left, along about ten or twelve feet, and soon I figured out that he had found an older trail, one that had fallen into disuse and gotten all covered up and grown over; and that was helpful, because even though the brush along that trail was still pretty thick, it wasn't near as thick as the regular brush, and it wasn't anything we couldn't manage. Too I noticed that we were getting into more hilly-type terrain, so that sometimes this old trail kind of looped up over the new one and gave us a solid and pristine-like view of it, so that other times it looped back down and we were back to being near flush even with the new trail. Well and along with that I noticed more and more outcroppings of rocks kind of dotting their way here and there, like a thousand years ago they'd fallen clean out of the sky and into that forest, like maybe from meteors, or maybe from some long lost planet that had come hurdling along and disintegrated itself against our world, leaving nothing but some concrete splinters; and me, I was taking to getting most relaxed again, and my mind was starting to wander away from Xamon and all its craziness and back out into my own far-off places, like thinking about playing my guitar, and even mentally practicing some of the songs I'd written; and too I was thinking pure crazy fantasy thoughts, like what it would be like when me and Mike, we had our band and were famous and known all over Nyala and the rest of Carbonia; when we had a little bit of money of our own, and maybe some cars and other such nice things, and maybe even some real nice girlfriends who fancied us for being so smart and creative, because truth be told I'd never had much luck with girls, never had much luck at all; and more specific-like, I was thinking about what sort of house I'd want to live in, and how big a yard I'd want to have, and whether I'd want one of those special couches that folds out all nice for guests who sleep over or just want to have an extra bedroom: a guest room, one might say.

Thinking on all those things was most nice and relaxing, and I was feeling kind of all-over refreshed and reinvigorated, and beginning to feel like maybe this whole Air Corps thing would work out okay after all, if we just had the patience to wait it out and get back to Nyala and putting together our band, when smack out of nowhere I heard a far-off rustling and crashing, like something was coming straight down the trail, and not coming slowly or in any way cautiously either; Mike, he must have heard it too, because he all quick-like dropped to a knee and sighted his M16 down over at the trail, and me, I dropped down too and did the same. Now as luck would have it we were pretty much in the middle of an outcropping of rocks when we took to hearing this rustling, and too we could see pretty straight and easy down onto the new trail; so we got down flat and flush behind a couple of big solid boulders, so that each of us was pretty well covered from fire, and from sight, and too so each of us had a real nice bead on the trail and anything that came down it, which needless to say put us in a much better position than we'd been in when we'd heard that earlier noise.

The sound of the crashing and the rustling, it just took to getting louder and louder, like quite a fracas might be coming, and me, I took to kind of tensing up and feeling all-over nervous again; but leastways we were covered now, leastways we might not get discovered where we were. And then in the distance I saw motion, first kind of blurry and sporadic-like and unclear, then a most solid vision of a figure coming toward us, running pretty much all out and bent to beat the devil; and I couldn't be too sure, but it looked like it was a woman, by herself, and my mind, it was trying to sort out all the sounds, where they were coming from, trying to figure if there were more people coming or if this one woman was making all that noise herself; but I couldn't sort it, not right there in the thick of it all. About the time she got a hundred feet from where we were hiding, the woman, she slowed up mighty considerably, so that she was walking fast rather than running, and too she took to looking back over her shoulder at the direction she'd come from, her breathing all hard and unsteady, like she was most near worn out and spent. And then she turned all the way around and kind of took to walking backwards toward us, not fast, but slow and steady and determined, like she was real-hard concentrating, like she was working

51

to will her breath back into normal-type breathing; and Mike, I could hear him muttering something not too nice down low and under his breath, and too I could hear him shifting around, and looking over at him I could see that he was holding his M16 skyward in one hand and working to draw his patrol notebook up out of his cargo pocket with his other hand; took him a few seconds to pull it off, but soon enough he did, and then he pulled out that notebook and took to thumbing through it, and when he got to the third sheet we'd been given that morning, the one about Digna Giraldo Cardona, he stopped and took to studying up the photograph real good.

And really there wasn't any reason for him to do that, because to me it was most clear that it was her, from the small frail-like body and the long black hair, and too from the way she held herself, that slightly tilting-forward angle that she had; yeah and even her clothes were similar, being as how in the picture she'd been wearing jeans and a long, loose smock-like thing, and now she was wearing jeans and a black button-down dress shirt; so me, I cleared my throat real low and quiet-like, to get Mike's attention, and when he looked at me I kind of nodded toward the picture, then to the trail, and Mike, he scowled real big and nodded back, not looking any bit too happy to be so close to someone we were supposed to be avoiding. I turned back to the trail, and meantime the woman, Digna, she'd turned back toward us and was kind of scouting around, still moving with that slow determined manner, starting now to look more calm, to breathe more normal; she was only about twenty feet up the trail now, and she seemed to be looking around so fierce and hawk-like that I was half afraid she was gonna spot us, so I tried to flatten myself down even more than I already was, and I could hear Mike right next to me doing the same. But still she didn't seem to see us, or leastways she didn't let on that she had; rather, she just took to coming closer, and then it became most clear from how she was walking that she was eyeing another little outcropping of rocks directly downhill from us, one that would put her about twenty feet off the trail compared to our thirty-five or so feet. And I guess she figured it was a good place to take cover, because all of a sudden she broke from the trail and made her way to it, quiet as a leopard and nearways as fast, like she'd been skating through underbrush all her life.

At that me and Mike both took to trying to get even more quiet, not seeing how we could do anything without attracting her attention, not seeing any way we could back on up and head on down the path without her full-on discovering that we were there; so me, I kept as still as I could and took to focusing good and hard down the trail, my M16 still perched where I could place some fire mighty quick-like down that way if I needed to; we didn't hear a single sound for a good three, four, maybe even five minutes, and all that time I kind of switched my glance back and forth from far as I could see down the trail back up to where Digna was hiding, and now I could see that she had flattened herself down behind her rocks as well, so that she was like a mirror-type image of us, only downhill a piece, only a heartbeat closer to the action. Yeah, and then out of nowhere there came the long hollow smack of a rifle being fired, M16 most likely, and to me it sounded far off and distant; but to Digna it must have sounded close, because she popped right up and took to glancing around, and I could see her dark eyes flashing something wild, and before I could have counted to three she was scrambling up the hill right toward us, and me and Mike, we just barely had time to roll a bit away from each other before she came spilling over our boulders and plopping down right between us, her face not a foot away from mine; and I declare that if I live to be a hundred I don't think I'll ever again see a face so full of surprise, and so full too of some kind of mixing of anger and fear and just all-over adrenaline. Mike, he right away reached over like he was gonna put his hand over her mouth, to keep her from making any noise, but then he stopped short, like he'd thought better of it, like he'd got a good solid glimpse at her face as well; and instead he took to putting his index finger up to his own mouth, and me, I just tried to ease back away from her as best I could, being as how it seemed to me like the brunt of her had fallen smack on me, and being as how even though she only weighed a hundred pounds, she was shoving my extra ammo magazines up under my flak vest and into my ribs, so that I was most uncomfortable and could hardly take to breathing without feeling a sharp, pinching pain.

"Who are you?" she hissed at Mike, her voice a whisper I could just barely hear, her eyes narrowing down and beading in on him, them thankfully not looking my way at all. "What are you doing here?" she went on, not waiting for him to answer at all, and for the first time she glanced back over at me, and her eyes were all-over fiery and accusatory, and me, I just kind of moved my mouth without saying anything, and then I tried to kind of smile, to show we weren't there to hurt anybody, but I guess that didn't quite come out right, because Digna, she real quick-like frowned at me and turned back to Mike, at the same time wriggling her body around so that she wasn't so near to being on top of me, but rather was lying flat beside me, and that took to giving my ribs some relief, and took too to evaporating that sharp, pinching pain the ammo cases had been giving me.

"Who's chasing you?" Mike, he asked her, ignoring her questions and trying to sound all firm and in control, his voice low and steady and just barely where it could be heard at all. Yeah and Digna, she opened her mouth like she was about to say something, and she left it open for a second or two, and then she closed it shut again and licked her lips, shaking her head and frowning, her eyes again beading down all dark and fierce.

"Tell me who you are," she whispered again, and then she kind of took to inching herself a little ways back from us, back from the boulders; not enough so that she was exposed, and not enough that I thought she'd get up and take to running away from us, but rather just enough that she could be looking at us both without having to move her head, and just enough so that it wasn't like we were all three so close up and intimate and such. I could tell from the way her eyes were running all over us that she was looking for markings on our uniforms, looking for something to tell her who we were and where we had come from, and Mike, he just kind of shook his head all disgusted-like, scowling up a storm, turning then to look back down

56

the trail. Me, I looked that way too, well because even though I'd been listening real close for any more gunshots--and so far I hadn't heard any--I hadn't been watching the trail too closely, on account of Digna dropping in on us, on account of how distracting she was to me. But far as I could figure the trail was still clear, and the woods around us too, leastways from anyone coming along at anything faster than a crawl. And I guess Mike figured the same, because he turned back from the trail and looked at Digna, shaking his head, licking his lips.

"We're not telling you anything," he whispered, "until you tell us who's out there trying to get you. If someone is gonna be coming down that trail spitting lead, we need to know who it is," he said, his voice all calm and quiet and slow, and then, just being Mike, he scowled again and added, as his own personal touch of sarcasm, "and we'd kind of like to know who they are before they end up sitting here in our nice little receiving quarters with us."

"Oh, I'm sure you'd know them if you saw them," Digna shot back, looking from Mike to me and then back to Mike again, her voice rising a bit, her dark eyes flashing all accusatory again. "I'm sure you all get paid from the same pot of money," she added, and then she took to looking only at me, and frowning hard and angling her face forward a bit, kind of how she'd been doing in the picture. And me, I took to feeling most nervous and antsy under her glare, and I didn't really want her being mad at us, being as how that didn't seem necessary, being as how we weren't really against her or anything, despite her maybe thinking so.

"We aren't gonna hurt you," I said, or rather kind of stammered, my words seeming to tangle up a bit as they came out, I guess out of nervousness, I guess on account of me feeling so intimidated by her and all.

"Eddie, let me do the talking," Mike, he snapped out real quick-like, not really in a mean way, but more in the voice he used when he was wanting to be real persuasive-like, when he was wanting to make clear that he knew best what we ought to be doing.

"So he's Eddie," Digna, she answered, looking my way, well and gesturing too with her long thin fingers. "And who are you?" she added, turning again to Mike, kind of cocking her head and angling it forward; and Mike, he scowled even bigger and took to muttering something not too pleasant sounding under his breath, and then he shook his head and took a long deep breath, like he was trying to calm himself.

"We need to know who is trying to kill you," he started again, his voice patient but also strained, it kind of showing that he was maybe not so much in control as he'd have liked to be. "That gunshot," he added, "who was that?"

And Digna, she didn't say anything right away, and when she finally did answer her voice was still defiant, but too it seemed to soften a bit, and she looked away from me and Mike and off down the trail, like in her mind she was taking to calculating something, some kind of complicated math problem or word puzzle. "I don't know. I thought they were still chasing me, but maybe not," she said, biting her lip, raising up a bit, like she thought that might allow her to see farther up the trail, or straight through all the trees and the underbrush.

"Or maybe so," Mike, he said, the sarcasm creeping back into his voice. "Would you be so kind as to sit back down so you don't give our position away?"

And Digna, she quick-like got real flat again, frowning at Mike and opening her mouth, like she was about to say something, but then closing it again and looking back at me. And me, I pretended not to notice her, pretended to just keep staring down the trail, because I wasn't about to say something stupid again, something that might give away more information about us.

"You're not from Xamon. You don't look like us at all," Digna said quietly, and truth be told it seemed really like she was saying it more to herself than to us, so I just kept to staring right past her, right down that empty quiet trail. "And you're not wearing the same kind of uniforms as the paramilitaries, or the Xamon Army, or even the Carbonia people at that air base," she added, and when she said "air base," me, I took to cringing a bit, not trying to but just sort of doing it anyway, and I guess my eyes must have wrinkled up just a touch, or my lips must have pursed, or my throat must have gulped, because she all of a sudden took to nodding and smiling a bit. "You are from the air base, aren't you?" she asked, and for the first time she touched me, placing her fingertips ever so lightly on my forearm, so that I could just feel her pressure, just feel her skin against the fabric of my uniform. And me, I glanced real quick-like down from the trail and at her fingers, noticing right off how long and elegant and lovely they were, how smooth and dark the skin of her hands was.

"Leave him alone," Mike, he hissed, shifting his body so that he was closer to her, so that he could have grabbed her and yanked her hand away if he had wanted to. "There's nothing you need to know about us. We aren't going to hurt you, we aren't going to turn you over to whoever is after you, we aren't even going to tell anyone we ran into you, so just leave him alone."

60

And Digna, she kind of recoiled a bit from the fierceness of Mike's voice, kind of leaned away from him, which of course put her leaning closer to me, so that I could feel one of her legs resting against one of mine, and could feel her shoulder flush even with my ribcage. She was silent then, like she was taking in his words, both his tone and his meaning; and it did seem there was a bit to digest there, being as how it was one thing to tell her we weren't gonna hurt her--well because that was certain enough true--and also to tell her we weren't gonna turn her over to anybody, because that was true as well, but I must say I was a bit surprised at Mike saying we wouldn't tell anyone we'd run into her, being as how that would go directly against our reporting back procedures, our "post-mission briefings" as they were called. It was one thing, far as I could figure, to make up a simple little cover story to explain us goofing around out in the forest for a touch longer than we were supposed to, but it was something else to actually run into something and not report back about it. So me, I kind of groped with his words as well, wondering if maybe he'd decided we weren't gonna report her back to our intelligence folks based on some of his earlier suspicions of where our intelligence was going and who might end up with it; either that or he was just plain lying to her, and I wasn't sure I liked the thought of that, so me, I hoped he was being truthful, but of course I couldn't ask him about it right then and there.

"So, if you aren't going to shoot me, or turn me over to anyone, or report me to anyone, then what are you going to do?" Digna, she finally took to asking, looking now only at Mike, and leaning a bit in his direction, her voice softer now, a little less what you might call confrontational.

"Nothing for at least ten or fifteen more minutes," Mike, he answered, looking away from her and back down the trail, like he was straining to see any kind of movement, too like he was listening as hard as he could for any little sound. "Look, anything you can tell us about who might be out there would be very helpful. Not just for us, but for you too; if you remember, it was you they were chasing, not us," Mike, he added, and his voice was calmer now too, like he was over his earlier anger, like he wasn't gonna let it keep him all dark and ornery any longer.

"So, you're really not with them? You're really worried they're going to find us?" she asked, angling herself forward, and her voice sounded different now, softer, more like the voice of a child than an adult, and chock-full too of some kind of desperation or hope, like she most wanted to believe what Mike was saying, but

62

just wasn't sure she should. And me, I all sudden-like felt like talking again, felt like taking to saying something reassuring and kind to her, being as how it seemed to me she was feeling pretty hurt and scared-like on the inside, and I didn't like to see that at all; yeah, but I kept quiet, remembering Mike's words, remembering too how I'd given out more than I should have earlier.

"We're not with anybody out here," Mike, he nearways sneered. "Just ourselves. Just doing our time and trying not to get killed. All I want to know from you is who are we likely to see, how many of them are there, and how likely are we to get out of here alive."

And Digna, she nodded at Mike's words, like she was taking them in, like she was working hard to absorb them and cipher out their meaning, and then all quick-like she turned to face me, and her eyes looked straight into mine, and they were so full of something deep and pleading that I most wanted to burst, most wanted to just stand up and run away rather than stay there and face her.

"Is that true?" she asked me, leaning nearer, so that now she was so close to me I could have kissed her, or she could have kissed me, had she had any such inclination.

"Yeah," I said, before I could stop myself, before I

could even think through whether or not I ought to be answering. And then she pulled back from me, but still she kept to looking at me, with those dark piercing eyes, like she was trying to see right through me, like she was trying hard to read words that were written on my insides, written real small, and real deep down, maybe in some fancy computer-type font, or maybe in some ancient long-forgotten language. And truth be told nobody had ever really looked at me like that before, never once in my life, and it kind of hurt me, in a far-off, mysterious, hard-to-explain kind of way, and got me to feeling all confused up and jumbled. I couldn't help but think that it just wasn't right that it was happening here, in this place, this rocky little outcropping in some nameless forest deep in Xamon, me all dressed up in combat fatigues and a flak vest and carrying an M16, instead of back home, back where I had my guitar, back where I was really me.

"Okay," she finally said, and she broke her eyes away from mine, and then she took a deep breath and looked back over to Mike, and shifted around like she was trying to make herself right comfortable before she took to talking. "I don't know how many of them there are. Really, I don't even know for sure who they are, but I'm pretty sure they're paramilitaries--SangreDenar mercenaries--at least that's what they were dressed like.

All black fatigues, nondescript, no markings. Like you guys, but solid black instead of camouflage. I'm sure there were at least three of them, maybe four; there could be more, but I didn't see any others," she added, looking first at Mike, then at me, then at Mike again.

"How do you know the paramilitaries work for SangreDenar?" Mike, he asked, only looking at Digna for a moment at a time, mostways keeping his eyes focused on the trail.

"Who else would they work for? My country's government may be corrupt, but geniuses they're not; they're way too incompetent to put together a force of paramilitaries on their own. If they could do that, why would they need you people here?" Digna answered, and seemed to me she had a good point, seemed to me that was the best explanation I'd heard yet putting SangreDenar together with the paramilitaries. But Mike, he just ignored her question and asked her one of his own.

"Why are they shooting at you?"

"Genocidaires," Digna, she said back, pronouncing the word quickly, almost breathlessly; and truth be told it was a new one on me, and I guess a new one on Mike too, being as how neither one of us said anything back to her; and Digna, she kind of waited, like she wanted to see how we'd react, then she went on. "You

65

know about the rumors? About the stories coming from the Saridita villages? You wouldn't be this far from your air base unless you were interested in all this, unless you were watching it for your government," she added, and now her voice was getting softer, almost like she was talking to herself again, and she kind of took to looking at me all intense-like again, so me, I looked away fast as I could, scouting through the underbrush, fishing for any unexpected movements. But Mike, he answered, still all low and quiet-like, still not looking at her.

"I'm telling you, we're not gonna mention running into you. Just help us get out of here alive and you can be on your way."

And me, I still was wondering if he was sincere on that one, and truth be told it was still bothering me on my insides, but you see what he said next was so Mike that I knew it had to be the truth, I knew that nobody but the real Mike would say it, and the real Mike wouldn't say it unless he meant it.

"We're just two regular airmen, lady, paying our dues and doing our time. We're here for our country, for our people; we're not interested in helping any paramilitaries, or in doing SangreDenar any favors."

And Digna, she smiled at that, just a little, and too she nodded her head. And then it was quiet for a few seconds, and then it was Digna who spoke next.

"How old are you two?" she asked, and me, I was most taken off guard by that question, and I guess Mike was too, being as how he looked real quick-like over at Digna, then at me, and from his eyes I could tell he was thinking on how to answer, wondering if it was some kind of trick; but then he nodded at me, like he was telling me to go on and answer for the both of us.

"Nineteen," I said, my voice still a touch wobbly-like, and I wondered if I ought to add more, elaborate, if you will, like by telling her when exactly our birthdays were, because I thought maybe she was wondering that, don't ask me why, but I thought maybe she was; but see Digna, she seemed satisfied with just what I had told her, being as how she was nodding again, nodding and looking back over at Mike.

"So he is allowed to talk sometimes?" she asked, cocking her head and angling it toward him a bit, and too cracking just a touch of a smile, and a most impressive one at that. And Mike, he just smirked and looked away, like maybe he wanted to laugh good and full but didn't want to let on that way, didn't want Digna to know he thought she was funny.

"Hey, don't be underestimating Eddie," he answered back. "Lots of people have made that mistake and most of them end up regretting it. He's deceptively simple,"

67

Mike, he added, and then he looked over at me and winked, and too he made that clicking sound out of the side of his mouth. And of course I couldn't be all the way sure or anything, but it seemed to me like Mike was paying me a compliment, so I grinned maybe a little and took to blushing a bit, and Digna, she just kept to eyeing me harder, like maybe she wasn't sure what to think of me and Mike, like maybe she was half-convinced we were a couple of outer space aliens, dropped clean out of the sky like the boulders we were hiding behind, human splinters instead of concrete ones. So then Mike, he took to trying to steer things back to the present, back to our predicament. "Why again do these people, whoever they are and whoever they work for, want to kill you?"

And Digna, she sort of lost her smile at that, which to me was kind of sad and a real shame, being as how I thought her smile most took to lighting up her face, most took to filling it with that spark of passion and vigor that I'd first seen on her in her picture; but see now she took to frowning instead, frowning and kind of knitting down her brow, like she was real hard concentrating, like she was gonna pick and choose her words most carefully.

"There's a village a little ways north of here," she started, "Ochoa, it's called; it's a Saridita village. A couple of days ago we heard a rumor that there had been a lot of trouble around there, a lot of paramilitaries around there, stirring things up and bullying the people there, and that's the kind of rumor that usually goes with the other kind of rumor that's been going around, the other kind of story that's been coming from some of the Saridita villages; so my two colleagues and I, we decided to make our way there from Xamon City to investigate, to find out what happened. We hired a taxi as far as we could, then walked the rest of the way on the trails. We got there this morning, and we had just started to look around. There weren't any bodies, but we couldn't find any villagers either. It was just like everyone was gone, like they all had vanished into thin air. Josue and Allende went to find the village elder's house, and I went to look for the village doctor. A few minutes later I heard people arguing, so I tried to go back to where I'd left Josue and Allende, but before I could get there I saw what was happening, I saw the three or four mercenaries dressed in their black, with their guns out, and they had Josue and Allende kneeling on the ground in front of them and they were yelling at them. Josue saw me and yelled at me to run, and I did. And they shot after me, and I thought they chased me, I mean sometimes I could hear them behind me, but I don't know. I really don't know. I just ran and ran and ran, for at least twenty minutes, and then somewhere along the way I hit this trail, and then I ran into you two," she finished, and then she just kind of stared at the ground and took to frowning some more, like maybe she was thinking things now that she hadn't had time to think before, back when she'd been trying to get away and save her life.

"I have to go back there," she finally said, not looking up, hardly moving at all. "I have to know what happened there."

After she said that she was quiet a long time, and so was Mike, and so was I. Mike, he took to getting a faraway kind of look in his eyes, like he was thinking and plotting out something, something right difficult and confusing. He wasn't looking at Digna at all anymore; rather, he was just looking out at the underbrush all around us, and occasionally up the trail as well. Me, I mostly kept to watching the trail too, though by now I was beginning to feel more convinced we weren't gonna be seeing anyone, and too I was pretty sure I'd been right in the first place, that the rifle shot we'd heard had come from pretty far away; still, it didn't seem like it could hurt anything to keep a good close watch out, just in case someone hostile took to approaching us, so mostly I focused myself on that, though I did take to stealing an occasional look over at Digna, who was still staring down at the ground, frowning hard and knitting up her brow again. Then Mike, he stopped scouting the brush and looked over at me, his face kind of screwed up into half a contemplative scowl, then he looked over at Digna, then out to the brush again.

"When you say bodies, that there weren't any bodies," he finally began, and then he stopped speaking just as quickly, but his lips kept moving, like he was trying to get his mind around something, trying to pick the words to bring his thoughts out.

"The stories from the other villages," Digna said quietly, leaning closer to him. "About the genocidaires. You don't know the stories? You haven't heard the rumors?"

"No," Mike answered, shaking his head a touch, then looking at me, like he was trapped, like he wasn't sure what she meant but didn't want to let on that way; and me, I thought about saying something myself, trying maybe to draw some more out, but I couldn't think of what to say, couldn't think of what to do.

"The stories are that the paramilitaries are massacring the Saridita," Digna began, speaking slowly, her voice nearways monotone. "Going to their villages and wiping them out. Not just rebels either; all the Saridita. Men, women, children, whoever they find. That they're doing it because SangreDenar is paying them to do it, so SangreDenar can get its wood, so the Saridita can't stop them."

"I can't," Mike said, again shaking his head, again licking his lips and searching for his words. "I can't see how that could be true. Not even SangreDenar would do something like that."

"Of course not," Digna said back, smirking a bit and looking off into the underbrush. "SangreDenar is from your country, mighty Carbonia, and we little citizens of Xamon are just ignorant savages, right? Just making all this up, right? Just bringing in all these paramilitaries on our own and making it look like they work for SangreDenar, just to cause poor little SangreDenar some image problems, right? Your compassion is overwhelming, mister unnamed soldier man," she finished, and for the first time she moved her body back away from us and took to sitting more upright, so that she was kind of kneeling, but leaning a bit forward too; and this time Mike didn't say anything, Mike didn't try to get her to lie back down flat; rather he just bit his lip and shook his head, then took to looking away from her, fixing his eyes and head on the trail.

"I don't know about all that," he answered. "I mean, it just doesn't sound right. And if it is true, why would you want to go back there? Why would you want to get into the middle of all that?"

"Again, your compassion is overwhelming," Digna said, and now her voice was getting a bit louder, her face was getting a bit animated. "I have to go back there, I have to know what happened there and what happened to my colleagues. This is my country, this is my home. And besides," she continued, "my food, my maps, everything is there; I didn't have time to get anything, I just ran. Just like this, just with what I'm wearing," she finished, and she kind of swept her hand in front of her body angrily, like to show what she was wearing, and me, I didn't really know what to say, or what to do, so I just nodded, just kind of frowned to show my sympathy.

And Mike, he turned back our way and sat up too, so that he was facing the two of us and not the trail, and he adjusted himself so that he was sitting cross-legged, with his M16 laid out over his knees and facing into the underbrush, his hands resting on it but not really holding it; me, I just instinctively sat up too, only I faced the trail, again kind of instinctively, or I guess maybe based on my training, so that we had both directions covered; I kept to holding my rifle a bit tighter, being as how I was the one still facing the trail, and too being as how maybe I wasn't quite so ready as

Mike to relax and give up totally on us having visitors. But Mike, he was occupied with other things, that was most plain from his face, from the kind of scrunched up and pained look in his eyes, and the way his lips were drawn into his mouth, and the way his jaw was set all nervous and hard; me, I wasn't sure what he was gonna say, or where he was going with his thoughts, but even though I was watching the trail, I listened up close just the same.

"I'm not saying that you're lying to us," he began. "I'm just saying that stories about SangreDenar ordering paramilitaries to massacre people, they can't be true, you must be hearing wrong."

And Digna, she opened her mouth like she was about to speak, but then she didn't; rather she just looked off into the underbrush again, looked off and took herself a deep breath. And Mike, he seemed to be watching her closely, like he wanted to convince her he was right, like he could see that so far she wasn't much convinced. So Mike, he kind of cleared his throat and shifted his weight, and she glanced back at him, like she was waiting, like she was willing to hear him out.

"What about this," he started, lifting his hands off his rifle, gesturing like maybe he was a salesman, trying to sell her big on some new car or something. "Me and Eddie, we've got some time before anyone back at our base is gonna be wondering about us, and this is our sector to patrol, I mean that's what we're supposed to be doing out here. So as for me, I'd be willing to go back there and prove to you that you're wrong, but only on one condition: only if we go carefully, only if we stay off the trail and go through the woods our way, the quiet way," he finished, and then he looked at Digna, and I did too; and Digna, she seemed to be taking in his words, seemed to be measuring them up and floating them around with her own ideas. And me, I was doing the same, trying to figure up Mike's motivations in all this, and trying to figure up my thoughts and feelings on it too. Part of me was still a bit worried, still afraid Mike had lied to Digna and was just wanting to gather information to turn in to our intelligence folks, but truth be told I'd mostly disregarded that idea, based on his words about not wanting to do favors for SangreDenar, and based too on just my general knowledge of Mike, of who he was and how he thought and what his particular take on this whole situation in Xamon was getting to be; no, seemed more likely to me that Mike wanted to go to Ochoa because he wanted to see for himself, to know for himself, that the things Digna was saying weren't true, that even if these SangreDenar paramilitaries might be mean and vicious to the rebels, still they weren't really going around killing innocent Saridita civilians who didn't have anything to do with the rebels. As for me, I wanted to know too, not just for myself but for Digna, being as how it was most obvious that this was something so near and dear to her, something that was paining her deep down on her insides, for herself and her two friends. And truth be told, even though I was a bit apprehensive about us heading up to Ochoa with those paramilitaries around, just in case her notions were closer to the truth than Mike's were, I took calmness in knowing she'd only seen three or four at the most, because not to be bragging, but I figured that if Mike and I did run into them, we could take care of ourselves just fine with odds like that.

"And if it turns out that I'm right and you're wrong," she finally said, looking all intense-like over at Mike, then at me, then at Mike again, "you promise you won't try to stop me from going to the news agencies? Because if I have proof that civilians are being killed, that's what I'm going to do."

"Hey, if you find out civilians are being killed, you go wherever you want and do whatever you want. Just keep me and Eddie out of it, just don't mention a word about us," Mike, he said, looking back at her just as intense-like as she was looking at him. And then she was quiet again, like she was studying on his latest words and weighing them up against her thoughts about us, about if she could be trusting us.

"Well, okay," she finally said, nodding her head solemnly, staring at the ground again. "I guess we can all go there together. But just so you know, I mean, I know I was running before, but I'm quite capable of traveling quietly through the woods. Believe it or not I actually have some experience doing that," she added, with just a touch of sarcasm creeping in there at the end, like she didn't want to seem rude but she couldn't quite keep from pointing it out, and me, I remembered how she'd darted off the trail and into that first outcropping of rocks, slick as a leopard, like she'd been born and raised in these here woods, so I took stock in what she said.

"Eddie?" Mike said next, ignoring her words and her touch of sarcasm and glancing at me, like he wanted to make sure I was up for everything he was proposing. And Digna, she real quick-like shifted her glance to me, and her eyes were still all intense and sad-like, but they were shining and hopeful too, with just a spark of that passion of hers, and truly it wouldn't have mattered what she wanted at that moment, I'd have likely as not said yes to it. So I did, and she smiled, but just for a second, and then she took to looking back at the ground.

"Well good; I'm sure this will work out well for all of us, and I do appreciate it," she said, real quick-like and quiet, and her voice it seemed to shake a bit, like she was feeling a lot more than she was saying, like maybe everything that had happened that day was taking to sinking in and being known.

"Don't appreciate it yet," Mike, he said kind of wryly, like maybe he was trying to lighten things up a bit, with half a smile and half a scowl. "If what you're saying is true, we could all be in for quite a day, you know."

Then he took to fishing out his map of the sector, and the three of us took to looking it over and getting a good grasp on where exactly we were and the general way we'd go to get to Ochoa, because we didn't intend on just going parallel to the trail anymore, but rather we were gonna swoop out far to the east, nearways hugging the border with Tyumen, and then make our way north from there, and then come into the village from the east; even though we thought that would add an hour or two to our plan, it seemed to us that was the best way to avoid trouble, and still we'd get to Ochoa with plenty of daylight to spare, being as how it was still just early afternoon. So then we ate a quick lunch, us sharing our rations and water with Digna, and then we set off, crossing the trail and

78

heading nearways due east, making our way all slowly and quietly through the thick trees and underbrush, Mike leading the way, Digna following about ten feet back, me all careful and vigilant-like covering our rear.

And come to find she was a most quiet and careful walker, truth be told more quiet even than me and Mike, with all our gear and such to lug around, and also because she just seemed to be light and natural on her feet, just seemed to move around through the underbrush like it was a stroll down a sidewalk. Took us a little piece of time to get clear enough of the trail and that whole area around it for me to start feeling normal-like calm again, which isn't to say totally relaxed, being as how we were still out patrolling, and being as how Digna's stories about SangreDenar's mercenaries butchering up Saridita villages were conjuring up some most unpleasant images for me. I wasn't completely sure how I felt, but I was tending to agree with Mike, I was tending to think there wasn't any way a company from Carbonia would be carrying on like Digna was saying, would be hiring its own private army to go and kill people, whole villages of people, just so they could come in and harvest up the forests around those villages. SangreDenar, they had a reputation in Carbonia for being greedy, for treating their Carbonia workers bad and locking them out or firing them any time the workers tried to up and organize a strike or anything, but seemed to me that even greediness had to have its limits, even greedy companies wouldn't be doing what Digna was saying.

But Digna, she didn't seem to be the lying sort, and I could most tell she was a smart and thoughtful person, so I had me some apprehensions, I had me some misgivings about everything I thought I knew about SangreDenar, and Carbonia, and what me and Mike were doing in Xamon. And seemed to me that maybe Mike was having the same thoughts, the same questions, being as how I'd never seen him as bristly and tense as he was as he led us through the forest. Truth be told I was kind of wishing he and I could just sit down and talk privately on it all, but of course we couldn't, not then and there; so me, I decided I'd try to put it all out of my mind, and though it took me some time I was finally able to get into something of a peaceful and contemplative-type groove, so that my mind was moving out and going in all kinds of directions. But go where it might, I couldn't ever seem to get too far from Digna Giraldo Cardona, first off from glancing up at her walking out there six or seven feet in front of me, but also just from thinking about her and wondering what she was really like; I knew from the fact sheet about her that she was about me and

Mike's age, maybe a year older, and I took to trying to piece together in my mind what it must have been like for her growing up, and I couldn't really picture it, I couldn't really piece it together at all.

Take for instance five years ago, when me and Mike were a couple of kids in Nyala deciding we were getting too old to just ride our bikes and kick around the old rubber works, deciding it was time to form us up a band, the two of us thinking all big and grandiose-like about ourselves and our future and what the world had to offer us; try as I might, I couldn't imagine what she was doing then, what her life was like, what her family was like. I wondered what kind of town she'd grown up in, whether she was from a rich, privileged family or something more like me and Mike, and too I wondered what her schooling had been like. Like I mentioned earlier, seemed to me she was pretty smart, pretty well-educated, and truth be told I was burning to ask her about it, and really I was just kind of wishing I could sit down and talk to her about all sorts of things; but of course I couldn't, not then and there, and sad to say, but even if I had been able to I'd probably have been so nervous and tongue-tied that nothing would have come out right anyway.

So me, I just walked on, frowning and fretting a bit on the unluckiness of it all, and taking too to thinking about my guitar, about my songs, wishing that at least I had my guitar there with me, so at least I could play her something I'd written, something real and pretty and substantial, something me, but without the tongue-tied part. Because you see, it seemed to me that whenever I was feeling kind of jumbled up and confused, or tongue-tied up, playing my guitar was right helpful, and the music took all those jumbled up and confused feelings and put them into a kind of order, gave them what you might call a sort of harmony in my mind. When I'd take to playing for a good long spell I'd get to feeling like everything that was stored up inside of me was running down my arms and into my fingers, and then through them and into my guitar, and when it came out of my amplifier it wasn't a big jumbled up mess anymore, but rather something beautiful-like and pleasant to listen to, something real and important and true. But of course I couldn't get out my guitar and play it, though leastways I could think about it, leastways I could run the rhythm of "Something More" over and over in my head as I walked along through that Xamon forest.

So I did, leastways for half an hour or so, and truth be told there wasn't really anything else out there to distract me from it, leastways nothing physical; no, the forest was most calm and quiet, almost eerily so, almost like what you feel before a great big storm takes to coming. Still, we kept to moving on, making our big loop out and around the trail, working our way to where Ochoa stood. By now it was getting on middle afternoon, and the day was taking to getting pretty hot, so every once in a while we'd stop and have a little break together, squatting down all three under the canopy of a big tree, keeping in close to the trunk to keep us covered. We'd maybe just rest a few minutes, or sip some water from our canteens, but we weren't able to really talk any, being as how we were still trying to be all quiet-like, being as how we were still concerned about running into something hostile out there. But even though we didn't get to talk, well I don't know, I still took to feeling like I was getting a little closer to Digna, getting to know her a little bit better, because when I'd offer out my canteen to her, she'd take to giving me that nice friendly smile of hers, and she'd always whisper a quick, quiet "Thank you," and too she'd sometimes keep to looking at me a little longer, like she was studying me, like she was trying to figure out who I really was, what made me tick on my insides. And of course that just got me to wondering more about her, about where she'd come from, what kind of place and what kind of family, and too what she wanted out of life, what kinds of things made her

83

happy and gave her pleasure.

Pretty much our whole afternoon was like that, calm and quiet and ghost-like stillness, leastways until we got within a quarter mile of Ochoa, because then my own nerves took to chasing away the calm and quiet and stillness and bringing back the stories Digna had been talking on, and judging from Mike and Digna, from their faces, from the increasing stiffness of their bodies as we got nearer, their nerves were doing the same; we had decided that rather than just walking right into the village, and maybe right into an ambush, we were kind of gonna sneak up on the village instead, sticking to the woods rather than the main trail from the east and creeping up as close to the outer row of houses as we could without losing the cover of the woods. Then we'd make our way through the village together, not splitting up like Digna and her friends had done earlier, and we'd keep together in a tight little group, so that we could all take cover together and then me and Mike could set up some kind of defensive fire if we had to; that was our plan, and even though it wasn't perfect, we couldn't think of anything better under the circumstances. Our hope, you see, was that the paramilitaries had moved on, either to keep searching for Digna or just to get on to more bullying in other places, but we didn't have any reason to believe that, other than just hoping for it; our worst fear, on the other hand, was that they had called somewhere and come up with some reinforcements, that all of Ochoa would be swarming with mercenaries in black, and that they might even have sentries out in the woods who might cut us down before we ever got to Ochoa, before we ever found out what had happened there.

So our little march was most light-footed and painstaking as we crept those last few hundred feet, with our ears and eyes tweaked up best we could, with any little movement in the distance or sound causing us to stop and crouch and make sure there weren't any people around; and when we got to where we could see the outlines of some houses just off in the distance, maybe three hundred feet from us, we stopped again, and Mike, he whispered that we ought to scan best we could for where we would place a DFP--which was military talk for defensive fighting position--if it was us setting up a perimeter around the village instead of them, so we could try to get in their minds and head off a possible ambush; so we scoured the area up ahead of us as closely as we could, and Mike even took to shimmying his way up a little humped-over gnarled tree, but we didn't see anything out of the ordinary, anything that might indicate that any paramilitaries were lurking anywhere around. Fact, according to Mike he didn't see anything at all, he didn't see the least bit of movement or signs of life. So the three of us, we kind of looked at one another and then moved on, then took again to working our way closer to Ochoa. And it wasn't long until we were right up at the edge of the woods, right up where the three of us crouching together could see a house directly in front of us and other houses all along both sides; and still there wasn't any sign of movement, and me, I was taking to feeling most strange and worried, most creeped out and eerie about what we might find.

"This is exactly how it was this morning," Digna whispered, staring straight ahead and pursing her lips up a bit.

"Let's just go," Mike answered, shrugging all nervous-like and intense. "Either there's something here or there isn't, so let's just be done with it, let's just go."

"You don't have to go any farther with me," Digna said back, and her words were softer, tender in a way, and her eyes were soft too, and she was frowning and angling her head downward. "You really don't."

"Thanks for your concern," Mike said next, with more than just a hint of sarcasm, almost like he was mocking her earlier words to him. "We're here, so let's just go."

And we did, but not the least bit hurrying; rather we

came out of those woods nice and slow and steady, Mike leading the way and kind of trotting up to the first house and then pressing his body all close up against it, like he was trying to absorb himself into it, and then he moved real slow and easy along the wall, and then he peered all cautious-like around the corner; and when he looked back, he kind of signaled with his eyes and with a slight little jerk of his head for us to come too. So Digna, she turned to me and shrugged, and her eyes were all sad and hollow and somber, like she wasn't sure she wanted to go, she wasn't sure she wanted to see what she was afraid she'd see, and me, I most lost my breath just looking at her; and then she was gone, trotting out the same way Mike had, pressing herself tight against the house and angling herself so that she was just an arms-length behind him; and me, I real quick-like followed after her, being as how I didn't see what good I would do in the woods, if something did happen, if suddenly someone did open up on us.

But it stayed quiet, calm and still and death-like quiet; we moved around the house and got to its door, which was standing open just a touch, like someone had thought to shut it but hadn't put enough arm into it; yeah and Mike, he popped it on open and swung himself inside, and me and Digna, we just waited right outside, me with my M16 scanning all the rest of the

87

houses, and Digna crouching not an inch behind me, so that I could feel her breathing close behind me, so that I could almost feel her fingers on my back, on my shoulders. Mike, he came right back out and said nobody was at home, but that it looked like people had left there in a hurry, because there was still food sitting on plates at the table, and too because it didn't look like anyone had straightened up or done any of the other things folks usually do when they're leaving home for a while. So on we went to the next house over, and we found the very same thing there: door a bit open, house a touch of a mess, food or knitting or other such things just kind of lying about; truth be told it was that way in every house we checked, strange and suspicious and downright troubling, and Digna, she took to frowning deeper and deeper, and finally after six or seven houses she just put her hand on Mike's arm and told him we should stop, told him we wouldn't find anything going on the way we were.

"If it's like the rumors we've heard of the other places, the other villages, they herded them all to the nearest open spot, the nearest field," she started, looking first at Mike, then at me, her eyes so filled with darkness that I couldn't tell what she was feeling, what she was thinking. "Let me lead now," she finished, and the way she said it was really more of a command than a suggestion, and Mike, he looked like maybe he was gonna say something, but then he didn't, and I didn't either; no, Digna, she was taken, sort of drawn up and mesmerized, if you will, and it seemed like she had made up her mind about something, and it seemed too that something was driving her, something was haunting her; and of course I couldn't be sure, but it seemed to me maybe it was her memories of places she'd been before, things she'd seen before, and all these rumors she'd heard about massacres too, and again I took to feeling an aching kind of sadness, at the distance between us, at how different and far off our lives were from each other, even now, even with us standing so close and it seeming like we'd shared so much. And too I felt an aching sadness about what we might find, and a jittery nervousness all tangled up with it. Digna, she moved on past me and Mike and took to heading for the edge of the village, the north edge, and me and Mike, we took to following close after her; still we clung close as we could to the sides of the houses, and still we listened all cautious and careful-like for sudden noises.

We made our way through the rest of the village, then down the main road north of there, and when we'd walked maybe a hundred feet down it we took to seeing a little clearing to our left, just to the northwest of the village itself; well and first it looked like that clearing was chock-full of boulders, like the ones we'd hidden behind on the other trail, but then looking closer I could see that these here boulders were small and odd-shaped and multi-colored, like maybe someone had taken a whole month's worth of washing and laid it all flat over just about every inch of them; and looking closer still I could see that I wasn't looking at boulders at all, but clothing, clothing and people, some of them lying alone, others lying piled together, but none of them moving. And for a second it was like I was struck from above, like I couldn't move or speak or even think, and truly I didn't know what to do, where to go, where to look even. Digna, she must have seen the people too, because she looked around real quick and sudden, like she was gonna dash across a busy city street, and then she took to running straight for the clearing, and me, I followed after her, not sure why but doing it just the same, and I could hear Mike coming along behind us as well.

But when we got to the edge of the clearing I stopped, and so did Mike, even though Digna, she kept going. Me, I was as close as I wanted to get, because now I could see the bodies close up, leastways the ones nearest to the edge of the clearing, and I could see their faces, and their eyes, and the bloodstains on their clothing; yeah, and it looked to me like most of the people had been shot--not that I'm an expert, mind you--but see, most of the people had two or three, or sometimes even four or five, smaller-type bloodstains in patterns going across their bodies, like maybe they'd been lined up and then mowed down, like they were so much wheat waiting to be harvested; and seemed to me they couldn't be real, couldn't be actual people, and long as I live I'll remember the expressions I took to seeing on some of their faces: the way their eyes were still open wide, the twisted-up looks of horror on some of their mouths, and the wide-open screaming looks on some of the others. And too I'll never forget the wide variety of people I saw sprinkled all across that clearing; they weren't all young men of fighting age--which is what you'd expect to find if they were Saridita rebels-- but rather they were the whole gambit of shapes and sizes and ages: there were children, some of them wrapped all clinging-like to the bodies of their mothers, and there were women, and men, and older folks too. Like whatever had taken to killing them was a disease, and not a very discriminating one at that. I can't say for sure, but seems like there must have been a hundred of them, maybe a hundred and twenty, and just standing there gazing out at them I felt like I was in a whole different world, one I'd never been to, one I'd never even known existed.

Digna, she was kind of walking her way through them all, like she was making mental notes, like she was scribing down in her mind every little detail, every expression, every bullet hole through every piece of clothing, and I tried to see her eyes, tried to read what she was feeling or thinking. But I couldn't start to figure it, I couldn't get a grasp on it at all. Now me and Mike, we'd been trained on how you didn't ever want to touch the body of a dead civilian, or a dead enemy either, unless you'd actually seen that person killed, because sometimes a body would be all wired up and set to explode as a trap, and me, I right then kind of snapped back to the present and took to worrying that some of these bodies might be wired up like that too, and I started to say something, even moving my lips to speak; but Digna, she wasn't touching anyone anyway, so I figured maybe she'd been taught the same, maybe she was being all cautious-like for just that reason, so I never said a word at all. Instead I turned to Mike, and I could see that he was most absorbed too in what was going on, most taken with horror and repulsion and sickness to the stomach; truth be told he looked like he might become physically ill, and his face was pale and kind of tinged with green, and too he seemed to be sweating all profuse-like out of his forehead. And the look in his eyes was one I'd never seen before, one of emptiness, like until just that moment he couldn't have even imagined this, couldn't have believed he'd see such a thing and truly didn't know how to start thinking on it, how to start processing it to fit in with everything else he'd seen in the world.

"We've been had, Eddie-man," he finally said, all quiet-like under his breath, kind of half wincing, half looking like any second he'd be sick. "We've been out here thinking we were serving our country, and really we were just serving this," he finished, and then he took to following up with some serious cursing, some serious calling of names and derogatory statements and other such things that I'll spare the trouble of repeating. Me, I looked back over to where Digna was, and I could see that she had stopped right by two bodies that were lying all tight together, a mother with her body draped all protective-like around her child, and now Digna crouched down, and me, I thought about yelling out a warning, about the wires and such, but still Digna didn't touch anything; and truth be told it didn't feel right to speak just then, even if it was to call out a warning. Meanwhile Mike, he turned away from me and walked a few feet back down the trail, and there shortly I could hear him getting sick, I could hear him coughing and spitting and retching. Me, I felt pretty sick-like in my stomach too, and the sound of Mike flushing himself all out wasn't doing anything to help with that, so I turned back to the clearing, to Digna, and I wanted to go to her, to walk out to where she was and tell her something: maybe like how sorry I was, sorry for her and all these people, sorry for everyone in Xamon, sorry for being there and coming from the same country as the people from SangreDenar; but I couldn't bring myself to do it; I felt too far away, too much an outsider, well or even an intruder. Digna, she had stood back up and moved away from the mother and the child, and now she was walking the clearing again, making her way to the next set of bodies, moving all slow and steady and methodical, like she was compiling her own personal catalog of horrors, and I got to remembering what we'd been told earlier about these Xamon human rights workers, about how they documented everything, about how they cataloged it all in case some day someone was interested in it, and I wondered if she'd ever seen things like this before, ever done anything like this before, even if on a much smaller scale; and I wondered again about what it must have been like to be her growing up in Xamon, what it was like before all the conflict started, and what it was like since then; and still I couldn't figure it, still I couldn't picture it up in my mind, though I was beginning to have more ideas, and beginning to feel a deeper-down kind of sadness.

I looked back down the trail, and Mike, he was still facing toward the village, still kind of bent over a bit as if maybe he wasn't all finished getting sick; me, I started to head over to him, but then I heard a cry, a shrill and kind of startled-like cry, and I turned real quick-like to Digna, and she was standing over a body with her hands up to her mouth, and again I felt like going to her, running to her, and again I didn't do it; the body, it was a man, and he was dressed different than most of the others, dressed more formal-like, in jeans and a button-down dress shirt, and I could see he wore a thick bushy beard, and all instant-like I knew who he was, all instant-like I recognized him from the picture in my patrol notebook; and Mike, I guess he'd heard that cry too, because now he'd walked over and was standing next to me, and he looked a little better, looked a little less pale and green.

"Is that one of her friends?" he asked, all quiet and solemn, almost like we were at a movie, almost like he'd come in late and was wanting me to catch him up on the plot.

"I think so," I answered, though really I was sure, and Mike, he nodded, and then we both watched as Digna crouched down beside the man, as she took to putting her hands on his shoulders and bowing down her head. Then she moved to the body next to the man, and looking real close-like at it--leastways close as I could from where I was standing--I figured it was the body of her other friend, and again she took to crouching down and bowing her head. And then she was up and moving again, walking on to the next set of bodies, continuing on with her chronicling of the clearing. But when she got over to a great big tall tree at the far edge of the clearing, Digna, she stopped, stopped and just stared at the tree with her hands dangling loose at her sides, and from where I was it looked like she was taking long deep breaths, like she had when we'd first seen her running down the trail, when she was nearly winded and all spent out; and then she just walked real slow-like over to the tree and kind of plopped herself down underneath it, so that her bottom was straddling one of the roots and her back was angled against its bark; and then she put her hands up over her face, and I could see she was shaking, and I could just hear a hint of her sobs floating on over across the clearing; me and Mike, we looked at each other, and I could see from his eyes that he wanted to go and comfort her just as much as I did, but I guess he felt just as far-away and alien as I did, because he didn't move toward her any more than I did; it was like for some reason neither of us could cross into that clearing, neither of us knew what to do or what to say or how remotely to conduct ourselves.

So Mike, he kind of cleared his throat, I guess to get my attention, and when I looked back at him, he kind of signaled with his head that we should sit down, that we should just take up a defensive position right at the meeting spot of the clearing and the trail and wait there for Digna to come back to us; and I couldn't think of anything better to do, so me, I shrugged, and then I crouched down beside him and took to scanning the trail for any signs of movement. Mike, he took to digging around in his cargo pocket, and then he pulled out his patrol notebook, and me, I figured he was gonna check the pictures we'd gotten that morning, just to make sure the two bodies we'd seen were Digna's friends, and of course I didn't see any point in that, being as how it was most clear that Digna had recognized them as her friends, and that she would know them better than we would any day of the week; but Mike, he didn't turn to the pictures, but rather he took to flipping through his maps in a right business-like kind of way, like he had something all pressing and important on his mind.

"You know, I've been thinking, Eddie," he took to saying, not looking up at me at all, but rather just

97

keeping to studying on his maps, his voice kind of slow and stammering, like he was distracted, like maybe he wasn't fully thinking the words he was saying, or else like maybe he'd been thinking them for a long time but was just now getting to say them. "When we get back home, when this is all over, we've got to completely change what we're doing with the band; instead of trying to find the just perfect bass player and drummer, we need to just find somebody and start playing, start getting out into bars and parties and playing our songs. Just stop talking about it and actually get out there and do it," he added, and then he looked at me, and me, I just kind of nodded, feeling most perplexed at his words, at how unfitting they were with everything that was going on, and even with him fingering through his maps and all.

"Okay," I said back, kind of quiet and meek-like I suppose, trying to run his meaning through my mind; it was good, I guessed, that he was wanting to get more focused on the band again, especially now, especially with him seeming to feel so used up and betrayed and confused by everything we were seeing in Xamon, but really I couldn't do much with it right then, really I couldn't really wrap my head around it and get any sense out of it. All I could figure was that maybe it was his way of dealing with things, his way of pushing away the bodies and the faces and the mouths all frozen open, pushing them away and trying to replace them with something better, something a little more promising and hopeful.

"I mean, right now we're just spinning our wheels," he went on, like he took my quietness for being unconvinced, like he thought he had to sell me on something. "You know, that songwriting contest, I messed that all up; that's what I mean by just spinning our wheels, just living on someone else's time, just waiting and waiting for some perfect moment that isn't ever gonna come," he finished, and he squinted down and looked at me harder, like he was waiting, like he was most interested in what I might have to say.

"No, I mean, I agree," I kind of stammered back, still sort of confused by the whole conversation, still not really sure what to think of it; and Mike, he nodded then, in a kind of long and thoughtful and drawn-out sort of way, and then he went back to studying up his maps, and he didn't say another word about it. And me, I just took to watching the trail again, still confused and half wondering if I'd just imagined our conversation, if it had really even happened at all; yeah and hoping too not to see anything down the trail, but feeling deep down that nothing that happened could surprise me anymore, not even the sight of a thousand paramilitaries marching in a tight formation and sporting a flag with the SangreDenar logo on it.

I guess five or six minutes passed, and still Mike didn't say another word to me, and then Digna, she came over to us, and she wasn't crying anymore, and truth be told you couldn't tell that she ever had been at all; no, her eyes were steely and hard and distant, and her mouth was pursed up kind of tight and angry-like, and she walked over with a kind of defiant stiffness, like she was deep down seething and angry, like she was afraid to speak for fear of what words might come out. But speak she did, fear or no fear.

"I have to go to Zadar, in Tyumen; there are news agencies there, international ones, and I have to find reporters who will get this story out," she said, her voice smooth and calm and matter of fact, her eyes glancing from me to Mike to me again; and me, I tried to look her deep in the eye, but she wouldn't do it, or maybe she couldn't, because her eyes still seemed far off and distant, lacking in the fire and the passion and the liveliness I'd seen in them before. "I don't have my maps, they weren't there, but I'm sure I can find it if you can just give me some general directions," she added, looking down at Mike, all purposeful-like avoiding my eyes.

"Do you think it will matter?" Mike, he asked her,

but he didn't look up from his map, he didn't dare to meet her eyes either. "Do you think anyone will do anything about it?"

"It has to matter," Digna, she answered back, her voice rising a touch, her hands taking to moving at her sides. "And someone has to do something. And even if they don't, I have to do something, I have to at least try to get the word out," she added, and now she glanced at me again, just for a second, and I could see that her eyes were taking to getting lively again, were taking to getting stirred and fierce and passionate, and then she looked back to Mike, but still he wouldn't look at her, still he wouldn't meet her gaze.

"Well, Eddie and I were just talking about that," Mike, he said, his voice all matter of fact in its own way, even if he couldn't lift his eyes up. "We were just saying how we sure were wrong on this one. How we sure got taken by the friendly folks from SangreDenar this time. We were saying too that maybe if word got out about this it might force SangreDenar to ease up a bit, to lay off on some of this, which would sure make our lives easier. So, you can see how we'd be interested in you getting safely to Zadar," Mike, he added, shrugging all exaggerated and nonchalant, and kind of furtive-like glancing sidelong at me, but still not looking up at Digna.

101

"So, you'll give me directions? Or at least let me look at your maps?" Digna asked, still staring at Mike, but then following his furtive-like glance and turning her eyes to me.

"We were thinking we'd go there with you, at least as far as we can," I blurted out, don't ask me why, being as how I couldn't tell you, except that it seemed like the right thing to say, the right thing to do, and too being as how Mike had me so up and confused with all his talk about the band, and about things he said we'd been talking about when really we hadn't, and so on and so forth that I was most jumbled up and confused myself. But I was most right away glad I'd said it, because Digna, she smiled a nice smile at my words, and her eyes flashed again deep with life, leastways for a second or two, and even Mike, he took to smiling down at his map.

"Yep," he said, "that's what we were thinking."

So the three of us, we took to crouching down and studying Mike's maps to figure out the best way to get there and how best to utilize the daylight we still had left; it was moving on late afternoon, and we knew there wasn't any way we could make it to Zadar by nightfall, being as how it was a good twelve miles or more from Ochoa; so we plotted up a course that took us pretty much straight east over to the Tyumen

102

border, at a point where we figured it wouldn't be too heavily guarded, and then from there straight north toward Zadar; we figured we could leastways put some distance between ourselves and Ochoa before it took to getting dark, and if we could find us a good spot to rest a couple of hours we could probably hit Zadar by dawn, even moving those last miles through the darkness. So we figured we'd head out right away, and then in maybe an hour or so we'd take a break and try some rations; yeah, and that last part of the planning was a touch tricky, because as for me, my stomach wasn't much for the thought of eating, not after being so turned and twisted by all those bodies, and I guess Mike and Digna were feeling the same, because we didn't harp much on our dinner plans, but rather we left them kind of vague-like and uncertain.

And me, I was most glad to get to walking again, to get to putting some distance between us and what we'd seen in Ochoa; Mike, he led the way again, then came Digna, then came me; we stayed clear of trails and such for the first hour or so, staying entirely in the trees and underbrush and such, but then it took to getting later, and we knew that soon we'd be losing our daylight, so we decided we'd track our way to the nearest trail on our map, and then we'd walk parallel to it but not on it, and too we'd try again to find some high ground like we had before. We figured leastways that way we'd be able to keep our directions better once it got dark, and too we'd have cover from anyone else who might be out roaming the trails. So Mike, he got out his map again and took to hunting up a trail, and then we plotted rough-like how to get there from where we were, and then we headed out, heading northeast at an angle that would intersect the trail in less than an hour; and it didn't take much walking to figure out that the terrain of the area was pretty much like that of the rest of the sector, with some flat areas and some hilly ones, and too with your occasional gully, and always thick with trees and underbrush.

The three of us, we made our way through it in silence, and much as I wanted to drift back to thinking about Digna, or playing my guitar, or the things Mike had said about getting going with the band, I just couldn't do it; no, my mind kept going back to the clearing full of bodies, to the faces of the people lying there, to their eyes; me, I'd never seen a dead body before, and never seen a ghost either, but seemed to me that those people lying in that clearing all sprawled out and contorted with agony came most uncomfortable near to being like ghosts, and I couldn't get the creepy feeling out of my stomach, nor the haunted feeling out of my mind. I tried though, I really did, taking to occupying myself with the things nearest around me, but even that didn't help much, being as how the whole forest was getting darker, being as how the late afternoon shadows from the trees were starting to fill the underbrush with pockets of blackness and uncertainty and a most general spookiness; yeah, and too my mind was racing with thoughts about SangreDenar, and the curses Mike had leveled at the people behind the killings, and where we fit into it all. And really I couldn't get very far with that, really I couldn't get a compass for how I felt about all that, though like Mike I was feeling a bit used up and betrayed and confused; plus deep on my insides I was beginning to feel a gnawing kind of worry, wondering what would happen even if we made it to Zadar, what would happen when we had to go back to base and pretend we hadn't seen everything we had. And really I couldn't get anywhere with that either, it being just a little too much, and it being more of a feeling than a thought anyway, more of a deep down uneasiness and tension than anything I could put words on.

Soon enough though we got to where we were almost up against the trail, and that distracted me a bit, because Mike, he found us a hill that he figured would let us look down on the trail and follow it along. Mike, he scaled it first, and I guess the grade on the side of the hill was pretty steep, because he had to pitch himself forward at a pretty good angle to scurry himself and his equipment up there; Digna, she went up next, taking kind of a running start and keeping her torso low to the ground as she went up, almost like she was ice-skating up it; yeah and me, I tried a combination of both methods, running and pitching forward, and that worked pretty well the first half of the way up, but then I thought gravity was gonna get the better of me, was gonna suck me back down to the bottom; but somehow it didn't, somehow I kept pushing and pushing and finally got myself up it.

And sure enough from up top there we could see the trail pretty well, which was good, though as Mike pointed out it also meant that anyone on the trail who looked over in our direction would have a pretty good line on us too; so we decided we'd have to be extra cautious, leastways until it got all the way dark, and even then we'd have to factor in whether the moon was gonna throw light on us and keep us visible all through the night. So that solved that, leastways temporarily, but real quick-like afterwards we ran into a bigger problem, because the hill itself was pretty rocky, and there weren't a lot of good places for a body to step, and it soon became most apparent that we wouldn't be setting any speed records if we stayed up there and kept to following it; so we pulled up short in a tight little rocky spot to discuss over what we should do, and we were just beginning to sort it out when Digna, she froze up all quick-like and raised up her hand, like to stop anyone from speaking, with her index finger extended and pointing upward; then she spun and looked down at the trail, her eyes getting narrow with concentration. Me and Mike, we turned that way too, both of us raising up our rifles and pointing them in the direction Digna was looking.

First I didn't see anything at all, or hear anything either, and I was starting to wonder if maybe Digna was just hearing things, was just a little too spooked from everything she'd been through that day; but soon enough I could see something far off down the trail, along about eighty or ninety yards down it, far as I could figure, though still I couldn't hear the slightest sound, and truly I didn't have a clue what had tipped Digna off that something was out there. Mike, he saw it too, and he all instant-like crouched himself down as best he could behind a boulder, so as to cut into our profile up there on the hill, and me and Digna, we followed his lead and crouched down there with him, with me right next to Mike and Digna right by my side. From up there we had a good view down on the trail, and come to find it was a person we were seeing, a person walking toward us; and come to find too he was dressed all in black--at least I think it was black, though with the fading daylight it might have been some other dark color--and he was carrying a weapon: some type of rifle, automatic by the thick magazine jammed up into it, though I couldn't say for sure the make or model of it.

"Paramilitary," Mike, he whispered, though seemed to me he could have spoken in his regular voice, being as how the person was still so far away; but about that time the person stopped and took to looking around behind him all careful and cautious-like, scanning not just the trail behind him but the underbrush too; and of course I knew it wasn't on account of him hearing us, being as how I didn't think there was any way he could have done that, but I must say it was right scary just the same. Me, I was wondering if he was alone, or if at any second we'd see more paramilitaries come ambling down the trail behind him; and for a second I feared we would, but then I got to thinking on it, and seemed to me he wasn't acting like he was with others; no, he was most slow and cautious, spooked-like, you might say, like he was all alone and knew it, all alone and not too crazy about it. Mike, he took to wiggling himself around a bit, raising his M16 up and fitting it on his shoulder just right, and me, I did the same; and then I took to looking through my sights, and even though the paramilitary had stopped and was still looking around behind him I drew a good bead on him, centering myself smack in the middle of his upper body. Mike, he seemed kind of fidgety beside me, like he couldn't get a good sight himself, and finally he turned his head and looked my way.

"You got a shot?" he asked, still whispering, still scowling out of the corners of his mouth.

And me, I thought I probably did, being as how I'd hit smaller targets from farther away when I was in tech school, but of course those were targets, not a real person, and truly I wasn't really sure how to answer Mike, what to say; I knew we weren't supposed to engage anybody except in self-defense, and it didn't seem to me that this was self-defense yet, being as how we hadn't been seen, and being as how this paramilitary didn't present us with an "imminent threat" as our instructors liked to call it back when we were in basic training and tech school; and I wondered if Mike had forgotten all that, wondered if he was that swept up in everything that was happening, and I was debating whether to mention it to him, and exactly what words I'd use if I did mention it, but I didn't ever get the chance; because you see Digna, she had some thoughts on this herself, and she took to speaking before I had a chance to do anything other than sit and ponder.

"No," she said, and even though she was whispering too, her voice was so strong and solid that me and Mike, we both looked over at her, and come to find her eyes were narrow and fierce, and she was scowling most worse than Mike was. "Don't you shoot him."

And Mike, he let out a strange little muffled noise, half like a sigh, half like a yelp, like he couldn't make sense of this Digna Giraldo Cardona, he couldn't quite fathom where she had come from or what she was saying.

"He's one of them," Mike finally answered, leaning closer to Digna, and me in the process, like the words he was speaking would be obvious to just about anyone at all, like he was most exasperated and confused that they didn't seem to be so obvious to her. "One of SangreDenar's finests. The bad guys, remember? The ones you tried to warn me about, remember? Maybe he was at Ochoa, maybe he did some of the target practice there," Mike added, his voice taking to being most vicious, and his words, leastways to my thinking, perhaps a bit too much.

"Doesn't matter," Digna answered, and now her voice was most mean and vicious too, so that it stung me, so that it sent a little shiver down me. "Don't shoot him."

And me, I was taking to feeling most uncomfortable being in the middle of those two, so I took to looking away from both of them, focusing instead on the paramilitary on the trail, though scoping him with my naked eye, not through my sights; and now he was full-on facing the other way, squatting instead of standing, his rifle drawn up in front of him ready to fire, like maybe he'd heard something most suspicious, like he was expecting at any moment to get attacked from that direction.

"Doesn't matter?" Mike, he asked, his voice still low but all thick and incredulous-like. "What kind of human rights activist are you? What about justice for those people back there?"

"Justice is fine; I want justice for those people," Digna began, and even though she was still whispering, her hands were moving quickly now, and her eyes were flashing, and she was leaning nearer to Mike, so close that she was almost touching me. "And I want accountability for the people who did that to them. But killing him isn't justice. Executing him isn't justice. Maybe he's a mercenary, a SangreDenar mercenary, and maybe he was even at Ochoa, maybe he did take part in that; but maybe he didn't, we don't even know that, and he is a person, just like you, just like me.

111

There's been enough killing around here already. People matter. All people matter," she finished, and she leaned back from Mike and crossed her arms in front of her chest, and I could feel her staring at me, I could feel her watching me, so I stayed focused on the paramilitary, watching him as closely as he was watching those distant woods.

"Can you hit him or not?" Mike, he asked me, and now his whispered voice was practically dripping with anger, with disdain, like if he could he'd just sweep everything Digna had said away and off the side of the hill, sweep it down onto the trail to be shot dead with the paramilitary. And me, I was surprised by that, surprised that Mike was taking to getting so agitated about it, because truth be told Mike wasn't really what you'd call a violent person; no, he could take to getting down and black and most grumpy sometimes, and hardly able to be tolerated, but he wasn't the violent sort, and truly I hadn't ever seen him take to striking blows or anything; so me, I wondered if him getting so angry, so focused on revenge, was just his mind's way of dealing with Ochoa, with what we'd seen there; was just his mind's way of trying to sort it out, trying to do something to fix it up and make it right, and maybe get back at SangreDenar while he was at it; and I could see how that could happen, how a body could take to reacting that way, especially if a body was feeling as duped and betrayed as he was, but I still wasn't sure what to think of it, exactly how I felt about it. So me, I raised my rifle and looked through my sights again, and quick enough I had the paramilitary trained up where I could see him, me centered again on his upper torso, though now of course his back instead of his front; and me, I thought back to the FTX, and again I felt that same strange calmness and collectedness sweep over me, and I was right sure I could make the shot, right sure I could kill him, if I were to pull my trigger. But see, I just couldn't do it, I just wasn't right with it; much as I respected Mike and usually took stock in his words, still I couldn't see how shooting that paramilitary in that situation could be self-defense, and even if it was, I couldn't bring myself to cross Digna, I couldn't bring myself to go against her will; there was just something in her words, and in the passion she took in her words, that took to swaying me over, took to making me believe that she couldn't be wrong about this, not with everything she'd been through, not with all she'd seen spending her whole life there in Xamon. No, seemed to me that shooting down that paramilitary in cold blood would put us about on the level with SangreDenar, not above them, and seemed to me that wasn't really something to be striving for.

"No," I finally answered Mike, lowering down my M16 but still looking at the paramilitary, truth be told not daring to look at Mike or Digna either one. "It's not clear enough."

And Mike, he just stared at me, stared at me and shifted around like maybe he was gonna say something else--I could see all that out of the corner of my eye, and I could feel it too, feel it in the air--but then he just let out a big sigh, like a father most disappointed in something one of his children has done, and then he took to letting out a pretty good little string of curse words and such, not really directing them at me or Digna, but saying them just the same. I just kept to looking at the trail, at the paramilitary, and before long he stood up from his squat, and after glancing around himself a little more he took to moving off the trail and into the underbrush, heading south, clean away from us, and pretty soon I'd lost sight of him altogether.

"He's gone," I said, and still I looked at where he'd just been, still I didn't dare to look at Mike or Digna.

"Of course he's gone, Eddie-man," Mike took to saying, and I could tell he was still a bit heated, but too his words came out a bit of what one might call whimsical, like he was relieved, like something of a weight had just been lifted off of him. "Let's just hope he doesn't go get some of his friends and come back

114

and find us, because something tells me he wouldn't have any of the moral reservations we apparently do, something tells me he isn't so convinced that 'all people matter,'" Mike, he finished, and then he stood up straight and took to scanning the trail, took to scanning the underbrush, like he was gonna make sure for himself that the paramilitary really was gone. And me, I stole a sidelong glance over at Digna, and she was looking off into the distance too, but off to the east, off to the way we still had to go, and I guess she could tell I was looking at her, because she turned her head back and looked at me, and it was a sad kind of look, not a frown, and certainly not a smile, just kind of vacant and lovely and wrenching, like she was tired, nearways over-tired, like there wasn't anything she'd rather do than just lie down and go to sleep. Me, I had to look away, because I wasn't sure I could stand that look very long, and truth be told I didn't know what I might say or do if something didn't take to distracting me right soon; and fortunately Mike, he right about then took to moving up out of our rocky spot, pointing himself east again, like he was surveying up the path ahead of us.

"Well, we might as well think up a plan," he began, turning himself halfway back to where Digna and I were still crouching, and his voice was calmer now, like maybe he didn't see any point in harping on the past, like instead he was all focused on getting through the future; just like he'd been when he'd given up on the songwriting contest, just like he'd been when he'd decided we were joining the Air Corps. "I think we should stay up here another two or three hundred yards, then I think we should just take the trails the rest of the way. We've got maybe half an hour of light left, if we're lucky, and we'll be useless trying to stumble around up here in the dark. We'll just have to be careful on the trails, just have to move as quietly as we can."

Digna, she didn't say anything to that, but rather she just stood herself up straight and took to following Mike, and me, I did the same. And it wasn't ten or fifteen minutes later before it took to getting most hard to see, the darkness settling in around us like a thick fog; so we angled down off the hill and worked our way back to the trail, and then we spread out a bit, Mike as usual up at the front, Digna following nearways ten feet back, me nearways another ten feet behind her. We must have gone an hour, maybe longer, like that, and me, I was getting most tired too, so that truth be told it was all I could do to concentrate on where I was walking, let alone to listen for sounds of someone approaching. I guess Mike must have been feeling it too, because before too long he stopped and crouched down at the edge of the trail, and me and Digna, we caught up and crouched there with him.

"I think we should find a place to sleep a few hours," he whispered, glancing from me to Digna then back to me. "We're gonna need to be refreshed when we cross the border anyway; we're gonna need to really be able to pay attention."

"Okay," Digna, she answered, and her voice was soft and quiet and far away, like she was almost asleep already, and me, I tried to see into her eyes, but it was too dark, and all I could do was make out their sparkle, and the edges of her face, the edges of her body. So on we went, Mike leading us a little ways up off the trail, up again to some high ground where we could bed down. We found us a spot between two trees, big thick trees that had to be a hundred years older than me and Digna and Mike all put together, and me and Mike, we took to digging out our ponchos and snapping them together to make us a little tent for camouflage and protection. When we had them all snapped together and propped up on some tree branches like a little lean-to, we took to digging out some rations, and all three of us set upon those most hungrily, even though my stomach was still feeling twisted and knotted, even though I wouldn't have thought I could eat a thing at all; then Mike, he said he'd take first shift on watch, and that I could take second, and then we just kind of took to getting ourselves set up for the night. Mike, he said he reckoned he'd better deal with nature, and then he excused himself for a few minutes off into the darkness, and when he got back Digna, she did the same. And while she was gone, Mike, he came and sat down on the ground right next to me, real close-like, and me, I was afraid he was gonna mention the paramilitary, me not shooting him, so I started bracing myself up real good and fixing up answers in my head to any questions he might throw at me, and too I took to feeling kind of nervous, because truth be told I'd never really gone against Mike before; I wasn't sure if Mike had an inkling I could have made that shot, but I was scared maybe he did know it, and I was scared too he was gonna say something about it.

But Mike, he was a million miles away from that, he was off on his own and pondering on far different things.

"We'll start by putting an ad in the paper," he said, like he was picking up right where we'd left off earlier, like not a thing at all had happened since we'd last spoken on this. "Not a big ad, nothing expensive, just something in the classifieds, something seeking a real professional-minded drummer and bass player, professional and solid and dependable, you know?" Mike went on, and me, I still wasn't sure what to make

118

of all this talk about the band, so I just nodded, nodded and shifted my weight around a bit, figuring this all had to have something to do with Ochoa, with Mike trying to make sense of it all, to sort it around and fit it into our lives.

"Yeah," I answered, "I can see that."

So then Mike, he got quiet again, but still he didn't move, he didn't take to getting up and moving away from me. Instead he just sat hunched a little forward, with his arms in front of him and his hands on his knees, his fingers hooked together to form a little steeple, his thumbs crossed to form a little x. And when he took to speaking again his voice was deeper, deeper and sadder and more hushed down and quiet.

"You were right not to shoot that guy," he said, "it wouldn't have changed anything. It wouldn't have brought back any of those people, and it wouldn't have stopped SangreDenar. Sometimes I just want to do what's quickest and easiest, sometimes I don't think things all the way through, you know?"

"Sure," I answered back, and I wanted to say something more, to show him I understood him, I understood he wasn't just talking about shooting the paramilitary, but really was talking about our band, and how he'd handled that, and our songs, and how he'd handled them, and us joining up with the Air Corps in

119

the first place. But me, I wasn't quite sure how to tell him that, how to put it into words, so I waited, figuring maybe he'd speak more anyway, and after half a minute or so he did.

"When we leave here Eddie-man, we can just forget all this stuff; we can just forget it like it never happened," he said, looking at me all intent-like as he spoke, nodding his head and licking his lips; and me, I wasn't so convinced that what he was saying was the case, I wasn't convinced at all that I could just forget Xamon, or Ochoa, or Digna Giraldo Cardona; nor that I'd want to even if I could, leastways on that last one. But Mike, his face had taken on a look of what you might call sadness, or maybe even desperation: a kind of unspoken aching-type look, I suppose one could call it, and seemed to me like he was trying to convince himself more than he was trying to convince me, so I just nodded back, just nodded and shrugged my shoulders and tried to look as reassuring as I could, even if deep down I had my doubts about what he was saying, and even if there wasn't any way I could express it to him.

About that time Digna came back, and she sat down beside me, sat down and angled herself forward so that she was looking at both of us, like she'd known us all her life, like she was waiting patiently for us to fill her in

120

on what we were talking about; and again I noticed that her eyes looked tired, most over-tired, with little black circles darkening in below them; and too they looked kind of worried, like she was afraid we'd been talking and had changed our minds, like she was afraid we were gonna tell her we couldn't go the rest of the way to Zadar or some such thing.

"Me and the Eddie-man, we were just talking about our band," Mike, he took to saying, his voice still hushed-like and quiet, but him trying to add a little something to it, maybe a little false enthusiasm or something, like maybe he could read her worry as well. "Just something we do back home, you know," he added, looking up at Digna and smiling best he could. "It's probably nothing you'd really want to hear about. Probably pretty boring to you."

"A music group?" she asked, tilting her head and angling herself back just a touch, and I could be wrong, but seemed to me that her eyes, they took to perking up a bit, took to shining, leastways just a little, with that spark of theirs; and Mike, he must have noticed it too, because he seemed to perk up a bit too, despite himself, and he shrugged and smiled and shifted around so that he was facing her more direct-like.

"Yeah," he started, "you know, nothing big, at least not yet; just something we're working on, just something we're getting started. I sing, and write lyrics, and Eddie-man, he's our guitar player, and my songwriting partner too," Mike added, glancing over at me, then looking back at Digna and kind of playful-like winking at her. "You maybe wouldn't know it, because he's kind of quiet, but actually Eddie-man is one heck of a guitar player; one heck of a guitar player," Mike, he finished, kind of stretching out his last words, like to extra emphasize them, him nodding too to do the same. And Digna, she nodded back, nodded and looked at me again, with that look, that piercing look that seemed to go right into me; and me, I kind of shrugged myself around and took to blushing a piece, glad mind you that Mike was talking up my guitar playing, but kind of embarrassed and all just the same. And Digna, she kept to looking at me for a few seconds more, and me, I tried my best to look back, though of course I could hardly do it, being as how even when Digna was so tired and worn down, still she was most beautiful and breathtaking, still she left me all unsure of myself and tied up in knots.

"Well," she said, still looking at me, taking to smiling a bit as well, "maybe someday I'll get to hear some of your songs. Maybe someday you'll write a song about Xamon, about me and the other people here. You know, we need more songs here," she took to adding, breaking her eyes away from me and glancing over to Mike, her smile fading just a touch, curling just a little toward a frown. "Less killing and more songs." And Mike, he just kind of half-smiled and shrugged, and then he looked away from her, looked back to the forest all around us, like he'd almost forgotten where we were, like he was just now remembering, just now waking from a nice pleasant dream.

"No argument here," he said, and then he stood up and kind of brushed himself off, and then he got to checking out his rifle and making sure it was all set to go. "So I'll do first watch, then I'll wake you up, Eddie; meantime you better get what sleep you can," he finished, and then he took to scouting himself up a good spot to do his watch from. Me, I stole another look over at Digna, and she was watching Mike, watching him and frowning a bit, her eyes again filled with their tiredness, her whole face kind of filled up, seemed to me, with tension, like maybe she wanted to say something else to Mike, maybe to apologize if her words seemed a little harsh at him, or maybe not. I wasn't sure what to say, or what to do either, so I just picked myself up and headed over to the tent we'd made, and when I got there I took to rummaging through my field pack, which I'd laid right outside the tent, hunting for my thin wool blanket; about the time

I found it and dug it out, Digna came over, so I handed the blanket straightaway to her, figuring she could use it and I would use Mike's, which he'd already dug out and laid inside the tent.

"Thank you," she said, taking it from me without really looking at me, without meeting my eyes at all; and then she moved past me and kind of scooted her way into the tent, and me, I laid my M16 down flat on the ground just outside the tent and took to following her. And the tent, it was pretty small, really hardly room for both of us at all, so I stayed pretty close to the opening area, to give her plenty of room, and when I took my flak vest off I set it kind of in the opening area, so that it was almost outside the tent, almost by my M16, trying to give us just a little more space. Truly the space in that tent couldn't have been more than six feet long by five feet wide, and there wasn't really room for either of us to stand up or anything. So me, I just kind of sat on my butt and tugged at my combat boots, figuring I'd leastways take them off and set them outside too, though of course I wasn't planning on taking anything else off, being as how I was in mixed company and all, and while I did that Digna took to arranging herself and her blanket against the far side of the tent, up tight against one of the big thick trees. When I finally managed to tug my boots off and shake them out and set them just outside the opening space, then I kind of laid myself down and pulled my blanket up over my feet and legs, even though I wasn't the least bit cold, and took to looking at Digna; and she had settled herself in facing the other way, with her blanket covering all her body and pulled up to about her chin, so that all I could really see of her was the back of her head, her thick black hair.

So me, I turned so that I was lying on my back, so that I was facing straight upward, and I was just beginning to go through everything in my head, all the crazy things that had happened that day, when Digna, she turned over, and me, I just instinctive-like turned my head toward her, and our faces couldn't have been more than a foot or so apart.

"Thank you for not shooting that person," she said, and she pulled her arm out from under her blanket, and all gentle-like she touched my shoulder with her fingertips; and me, I was most mortified and uncertain what to say, with her touching me like that and all, so I just laid there, trying to figure if a "you're welcome" would be appropriate, staring at the sight of her long thin fingers resting on my uniform, trying somehow to put that sight into my memory, so that I could call it up later, remember that it was real and true maybe if everything else about Xamon was faded or gone. And

Digna, she squeezed my shoulder, just a touch, just with the tip of her thumb and the tip of her index finger, and then she lifted up her hand and pulled her blanket back up tight, and then she turned over and faced the tree again. "Good night," she said, or rather whispered, so that I could barely hear her.

"Good night," I said back, and then I turned and propped myself up on my elbow, and I thought about saying something else to her, something grand and elegant and maybe even profound, but I couldn't think of anything, I didn't remotely know what I ought to say; so instead I just eased myself back to lying down, still facing her though, facing her and watching her blanket rise and fall with her breathing. Soon enough I could tell she was asleep, from the evenness of her breathing, from the stillness of her body. And still I couldn't think of what I'd say, even if she were awake to hear it.

So me, I just laid back down flat and stared up at the ceiling of the tent, and I could just make out the changes in the camouflage, could just make out the lines that formed the edges of the pattern; and as I stared up at the ceiling, my mind took to going back over the day, and all the crazy things that had happened, because even though my body was feeling most tired, still my mind wasn't ready to quit yet, wasn't ready to shut down and relax until it had worked through a few things, until it had screened them and sorted them the best it could. I tried to think about the pleasant things from the day, like having Digna smile at me, and having her touch my shoulder there in the tent, and having Mike compliment me on my guitar playing right in front of Digna, and too having Mike talk about us taking a new approach to the band when we got home; and those things were nice, most nice and comforting, but really my mind wouldn't stick to them, really my mind didn't want to spend its time on those things. Rather it just kept coming back to Ochoa, to that little clearing so all-over littered up with bodies of people, and the expressions on those people's faces, and the tangled up and contorted-like positions their bodies were lying in, and the mothers, and the children, and all the little bloodstain patterns so neat and even-like across their clothing; and too the way Digna had walked through the clearing and looked at them all, and the sound she'd made when she'd discovered the bodies of her friends--Josue and Allende, she'd called them--and the way she'd sat down and cried. Too I took to thinking about that paramilitary, about how I could have shot him, killed him most likely, and about how Digna had felt so strongly that I shouldn't, even if maybe he had been at Ochoa, even if maybe he had helped with all the killing there. My mind, it took to trying to sort through it all and make it all make sense, but too I guess my tiredness was kicking in, because soon enough it seemed to me like everything kept getting all twisted up and confused, so that in my mind I was seeing that paramilitary lying dead in the clearing in Ochoa, and I was seeing those tangled up bodies spread all over the village of Ochoa, instead of out in that clearing, and I was seeing Josue and Allende traveling down a Xamon trail, their bodies bloodied but them not dead, the two of them having some kind of far-off and distant conversation, something about Digna, about finding her and taking her home; more and more all those thoughts took to getting mixed together, until I could hardly tell if I was awake or dreaming, if my thoughts were memories or just fanciful wanderings of my mind.

Well somewhere in the middle of it all I must have drifted off into something like being asleep, though I couldn't have said for sure when or how, because all of a sudden out of nowhere my mind popped back to being all the way awake again, awake and feeling a painful-like gripping on my shoulder, most squeezing it down like a teacher crushing up a piece of chalk or something; and for a second I thought it was Mike, waking me to tell me it was my time on watch, and I was starting to feel most irritated that he would grab me so hard, but then I got my eyes open and adjusted-up to the darkness again, and I realized that I was lying on my side facing Digna, and that she was facing me, and that it was her that was squeezing me so hard, that her right hand was draped over me and squeezing down on my left shoulder. She wasn't awake, leastways she didn't appear to be; rather, she seemed to be deep in a sleep, maybe deep in a dream, and from the look on her face and the squeezing on my shoulder, it didn't seem like it was a good dream either; no, in her sleep her face had taken to looking most beaten down and tragic, in a way I hadn't ever seen her look when she was awake, so that her eyebrows were knitted up all tense-like, and her eyes were scrunched closed all tight and quivery, and her lips were creased straight and kind of twitching a bit; too her teeth were moving, them kind of grinding against one another, and me, I was most certain that she must have been having some kind of nightmare, some kind of sad and miserable and frightful-like nightmare, and I wondered if I should try to wake her up, just to bring her out of it, just to give her some relief from it. Well and to give myself some relief from it too, because truth be told her squeezing was taking to aching up my shoulder something fierce.

So me, I tried to angle my body away from her, tried to kind of slither, if you will, my shoulder down and out from under her grip, so that I could try to gently-like shake her awake; but see, I couldn't quite get out from under it, being as how it seemed like every time I moved my shoulder, her hand, it moved with me, like it wasn't gonna let go, so that the bones of her long slim fingers kind of flexed and pivoted with every move I made; me, I switched gears a bit, reaching up with my right hand and trying to lift her hand loose, and at the same time trying to move my shoulder back and away from it. That worked better, and finally I was able to get her hand lifted, and her fingers, they loosened up quite a bit once they were off my shoulder, so that her hand felt soft and smooth and somehow fragile when I held it in my hand; and me, I kind of took her hand in both of mine and then set it down real gentle-like in the space between us, and I started to let go of it, to leave it there on its own, but instead I just kept to holding my hand over it, just kept to feeling the softness of her skin and the smoothness of her bones.

Digna, she seemed to ease up a bit at that, and her shoulders, they kind of shrugged a little, while her head, it kind of nudged itself around a little, and her eyebrows, they weren't so tight and tense-like, and her lips, they kind of eased themselves almost into a smile; I guess I knew deep down on my insides that it was wrong to keep touching her hand that way, when she was asleep, like I was anything more than someone she'd just met that very day, but too I saw how it seemed to be helping her, comforting her, even if she was asleep, and truly I didn't see how it was hurting anything, not in the great big grand scheme of things, not in the world of Xamon and Carbonia and SangreDenar and the like. And truth be told seeing Digna sleeping so painful and distraught had kind of taken me to wondering how long a person could stay like Digna in a place like Xamon; how long a person could stay so vibrant and life-loving and resilient-like all the time, with such a breathtaking smile and such a flash in the eyes; how a person could keep getting up every day and wanting to face a place where things happened like what we had seen in Ochoa. And too I wondered how many Ochoas one person could handle, how many walks through clearings scattered with bodies one person's mind could take in and process before finally that mind took to shutting down, took to saying thanks but no thanks to functioning in any kind of normal-type way; how long it would be before a person like Digna took to being just as tensed-up and jilted when awake as she had been when she was asleep; and too how long it would be before even a person like Digna gave up on believing that all people mattered.

131

That got me to thinking about the future, not like a week or a month away, mind you, but the big future, the long-term future; like five years down the road, like ten, like twenty; and me, I tried to picture up in my mind what Digna would be like in five years, what her life would be like if she kept to being a human rights activist in Xamon, and if things in Xamon didn't get any better, if even after she found her some reporters and got them to go to Ochoa and tell the world about what had happened there nothing changed; if the world didn't take to caring, if SangreDenar didn't take to changing, if the Carbonia government didn't take to putting the skids on SangreDenar; and I couldn't picture it, leastways not in any remotely positive kind of way. No, it was more like trying to picture her past, trying to picture what her childhood had been like, and her parents, and her friends and her school and just her life in general; and just like I couldn't seem to conjure up anything about those things, too I couldn't see anything clear in my mind about her future, about what she'd do even a week down the line, when everything really took to sinking in, everything from Ochoa, everything about her friends Josue and Allende. I guess it was late, and just kind of an all-around whirlwind sort of day, because then my mind took to really wandering, and I took to thinking all sorts of crazy-type

132

notions, like what it would be like if me and Digna, we were married, married and living together somewhere way far away from Xamon, or Carbonia, don't ask me where, or what it would be like if me and her and Mike all three went to the Tyumen government in Zadar and asked for some kind of political or humanitarian asylum--never mind how Mike and I would make it anywhere in Zadar in our uniforms, because my mind wasn't really interested in pondering on that--and what would happen next, and where we'd go, and other such nonsense that my mind wouldn't have tolerated for one second in the light of day. And I guess somewhere in the middle of all that thinking I drifted off into sleep for real, because next thing I knew I was being pulled on the shoulder again, only this time there wasn't any squeezing, but rather just a shaking, a firm but easy over-and-over again kind of shaking; and too there was a voice, Mike's voice, whispering in a quick almost panicked sort of way.

"Eddie-man, we've got to get up and get going," he was saying, his hand still taking to shaking a rhythm on my shoulder, his face poked into the tent so that it was just inches from mine. "I fell asleep, Eddie-man, we've been here close to four hours," he added, and me, I tried to take in what he was saying, but truth be told I was kind of off in a mixed-up and confused state of my

133

own, with my mind still racing with thoughts of being married to Digna, and too with memories of Ochoa and the rest of the day, and now with real-life sensations like Mike's hand on my shoulder and a kind of tightened-up cramping in my legs--most likely from all the walking we'd been doing--and a dryness in my throat and a soreness in my back from the hardness of the ground. So me, I just kind of sat up and nodded, hoping leastways that would get Mike to quit his shaking, and then I took to looking around and trying to get my bearings; Digna, she was still sleeping, and I guess sometime in the night she must have taken her hand back, or I must have lifted mine off of it, because now she was turned back away from me and toward the tree, and her hands were both buried down beneath her blanket. So me, I turned back to Mike, and by now he had stopped shaking my shoulder, but he still had his hand on it and he was still looking at me all intense-like.

"We've only got a few more hours of darkness," he added, nodding and licking his lips, like to hurry me up, like to goad me on.

"All right," I answered, nodding back, and I figured I'd better take to waking Digna, so that we could get up and moving again, though truly I wasn't sure I wanted to, being as how she seemed to be sleeping so peaceful-like and all; but I couldn't see how I had much choice, considering the time we'd lost already, so I reached over and took to shaking her shoulder real gentle-like and slow, thinking to myself that it wasn't at all like Mike to fall asleep on watch, and thinking too that it was a good thing nobody--leastways nobody with hostile intent--had come ambling up on us while we were all three sleeping. Mike, he drew himself on back out of the tent, and Digna, she took to stirring around and awake pretty quick-like, and then she turned over and faced me, and for a moment her eyes looked kind of spooked-like, kind of startled, but then real quick they took to being all sharp and black and filled with life again, like she had been most recharged by sleeping, and her lips, they were kind of parted into an expression of excitement, or maybe just contentment, like she couldn't wait to get back to living, she couldn't wait to see what life would bring her next. Me, I was glad to see that expression, it made me feel better, leastways a little, and too it took to erasing away some of my memories of how she'd looked during her nightmare.

"Is it time already?" she asked me, glancing around, aware, I'm sure, of the darkness both in and outside the tent. And me, I said it was, though I left out the part about Mike falling asleep, being as how I didn't see how that was important now, since we hadn't been ambushed or anything; Digna, she sat up and let her blanket kind of fall down off her shirt and down about her waist, and then she clasped her hands together and stretched them out in front of her, toward her feet, and me, I slid on out of the tent and gathered up my boots, figuring I'd give her some space to get herself up and awake. It was still right dark outside the tent, but me, I kind of shook my boots and dumped them out anyway, even though I knew I probably wouldn't see anything that fell out of them, but feeling like I ought to shake them out before I put them back on just the same, just in case some creature had taken to living in them while I was sleeping; next I slid my feet into them and laced them back up, then I gathered up my flak vest and put it back on, then I slung my M16 over my shoulder and took to helping Mike gather up everything to put back in our field packs. Digna came out of the tent too, carrying both the blankets, and then she helped us fold them back up and put them in the field packs; next we all took to taking down the tent, then unsnapping the ponchos from one another and folding them up, getting them all put away as well. After that we took to policing up the area as best we could in the darkness, so that nobody would be able to tell we'd been camped there, so that the area would be just as free and wild and pristine-like as it had been when we'd found it.

Soon enough we were ready to go, and we worked our way back down to the trail and took to our regular travel pattern, Mike up front, then Digna, then me. I was glad to be moving again, because truly it did seem like walking a trail always took to freeing up my mind from troubles and getting me to feeling good and calm and easy again, even walking a trail on patrol; my mind took to wandering again and going over all my night-thoughts and dreams, and I have to admit I blushed up and cringed a bit to myself--of course neither Mike nor Digna could see me, being as how they were walking in front of me, and I was most thankful for that--when I thought on how I'd been picturing me and Digna married, because in waking thoughts it seemed most silly, most childlike and foolish and fanciful. But still, I got to admit that as we walked along in the darkness I took to pondering on it a little bit again, just a little, and truly it wasn't a disagreeable thought in the least, only problem being that I couldn't ever quite figure out how the particulars of something like that might happen, her and me getting married that is, not with all the meddling the real world seemed to be doing in our affairs. So me, I just had to let it go, leastways for the time being, but I sure didn't want to think about Ochoa, I sure didn't want to see again in my mind what I'd seen there, so instead I just pushed my mind best I could to wandering away to my guitar, to a new song I was starting to work up in my head; it was gonna be long and slow and full of feeling--all drawn-out and mournful, you might say--kicking off with a blazing riff of clear crisp high notes, followed up with some pretty heavy chords, soaked a bit in tremolo and reverb; exactly which notes and chords I hadn't figured out yet, but I was working on it, leastways working best I could without having my guitar there to try things out on. And thinking on the song was good, was calming and relaxing and kept me far from Ochoa.

On we went, ending up crossing the border into Tyumen sometime about an hour before sunrise, leastways best we could tell; truth be told we weren't sure exactly when we made it into Tyumen, being as how our maps just showed a big open area, which seemed to us to be just about right, being as how there weren't any markings out there deep in the forest to signify the borders, and too being as how we'd purposely avoided the border crossing checkpoints that a body was supposed to use, the ones that were marked up on our maps. Once we were across we took to heading due north, straight for Zadar, figuring we'd still make it there before the day got too far along; figuring too that me and Mike, we'd walk with Digna as close in as the forest would let us, and then we'd have to stop, and then it would be up to Digna to blend herself in to the little villages on the outskirts of the city all on her own, being as how there wasn't any way me and Mike could be coming out of the forest in our uniforms and with our weapons, not without causing some kind of international incident. And far as Digna blending in, we didn't think that was gonna be any problem, being as how people from Tyumen and people from Xamon were right similar in a lot of ways, from features to language, to clothing, to just their ways of doing things in general; and too being as how Digna was pretty sharp on those kinds of things, and pretty sharp at thinking on her feet as well, if the need were to arise.

So we kept to walking, and along about the time the sun took to peeking up in the distance, we took to studying up our maps again, and seemed like we had to be getting right close to Zadar, though we couldn't tell yet, though still the woods were thick and obscuring; still, we took to doubling up our pace best we could, knowing that we weren't likely to run into any paramilitaries in Tyumen, and that really our main concern was just keeping from being seen by the locals and such. Before long we got to where we could see a long broad clearing up ahead of us, and we figured it most likely marked the beginning of the outskirts of Zadar, the first break in the woods that opened on up into a village, so we hurried ourselves to the edge of the clearing and then crouched down and stopped. And me, I don't know, I was taking to feeling most jumbled up and confused, because on the one hand I was feeling most happy and relieved that we'd made it to where we were, that we'd managed to get ourselves to the edge of Zadar without getting killed; but on the other hand, I was also taking to feeling a certain kind of deep down sadness, that Digna would be going soon, and that we wouldn't be going with her; and too that maybe I wouldn't be seeing her again, maybe even ever. I didn't really know what to do with those feelings, I didn't know where to put them, so I just tried the best I could to keep them all on the inside, buried deep down with my visions of Ochoa, and to keep myself focused on our mission and on getting things done.

Digna, she seemed right focused herself, because you see, I was watching her most closely, and I could tell by the way she was looking all serious-like in her face, and was carrying herself all angled forward and ready to go, that she had figured herself up a plan, that she was plum sure of what she needed to do and how she should go about doing it. And I was glad of that, I truly was, because I knew deep down that was the most important part, that Digna went and found her some reporters, and that word got out to the world about what had happened in Ochoa; but too those other feelings kept trying to come back up, and I couldn't help but feel like I was losing something, something nobody ought to have to lose.

Now Mike, he seemed to be feeling good himself, light and free and easy, like he was most unstressed and relieved, like he'd worked some things through in his mind and come to some kind of peace with himself about them; like maybe he'd made some kind of deal with himself about getting Digna to Zadar, and now was most glad he'd been able to keep his end of it, most glad he'd been able to do something to help get the word out to the rest of the world about Ochoa. Seemed to me he was practically skipping by the time we reached that clearing, and he was grinning all big and outright, and he seemed to be most pumped up and excited; and me, I was happy for him, and for me, being as how things were always better if Mike was up and jovial and ecstatic-like, rather than down and gray and gloomy--which as you know by now he could sometimes take to being--but too I was a little concerned, since he and I still had to track our way all the way back to the base without running into trouble. And too since I couldn't see how we were gonna be able to go back to the base and act like nothing had happened, act like we were still ignorant of everything SangreDenar was up to in Xamon. Or that we should act that way, even if we could. But thinking on all that was just too much for me right then, with all my other thoughts about Digna swimming so crazy in my mind, with the three of us sitting crouched together looking out at the clearing.

"Well, I guess this is where we part ways," Digna said, smiling and nodding, looking first at Mike, then at me, then at Mike again. "I really appreciate what you did, both of you," she added, and she nodded a little extra in Mike's direction, and me, I figured it was maybe something of a peace gesture on her part, maybe to make up for the times when she might have been a little hard on him; and Mike, he kind of shifted around and smiled a touch and nodded back.

"Yeah well just remember," he said, grinning kind of sheepish-like and making his clicking noise as well, "to keep Eddie and me out of the news." And Digna, she smiled at that, smiled in a reserved kind of way and then sort of dropped her eyes, and then she nodded again and licked her lips.

"Absolutely," she said, "you have my word." Well and then she kind of reached out her hand in a sort of awkward-like way, kind of stiff and formal, and Mike, he took her hand and shook it, like they were making a deal, like they were standing in an office somewhere rather than crouched down at the edge of a clearing. And then Digna, she turned to me, still with her hand out, and she smiled that smile that was so fetching on her, so enchanting and bedazzling, and too her eyes looked right into mine, and me, I just kind of leaned over and hugged her, best I could without losing my balance and tipping us over, and Digna, she hugged me back, tightly, almost as tightly as she'd been holding my shoulder in the middle of the night; and me, I didn't want to let go, I didn't want to let her stand up and walk away. My mind raced with thoughts of what I should say, or what I should do, but none of those thoughts would come clear, none of them would settle down and make sense, so I just kept to crouching there, not really doing a thing at all.

"Be careful," I finally said, and Digna, she hugged me for a moment longer, patting my back in a friendly kind of way, and then she pulled herself away, and for just a second before she stood back up she took to looking in my eyes again, one last time with that piercing look of hers.

"Thank you," she said, "you've been very kind to me, Mr. Eddie-whoever-you-are." Seemed to me like she was gonna say something more, leastways she kept to looking at me, looking into me, but then she just smiled real big and kind of shrugged her shoulders and tilted her head, and next thing I knew she was up and gone, trotting off into the clearing, and after that she didn't look back at us at all.

But me, I kept to looking after her, watching as she got farther and farther away, as she got smaller and smaller off in the distance. Wasn't long before she was out of shouting range, so far away that even if I'd tried to I couldn't have called her back, even if I'd thought of something to say; and then she was gone entirely, disappearing behind the first row of houses in the village. Mike, he asked me if I was ready to go, and his voice was kind of quiet, and I could tell by his tone and by the look in his eyes that he'd been watching me for a long time, watching me as I watched Digna, and that he'd been waiting patiently for me, much as he was bursting with excitement and ready to get on and start heading out of there, in the straightaway pattern he'd laid out, in a way that didn't take us anywhere near Ochoa.

"Sure," I answered him, and we stood up and turned back toward the forest, and Mike, he added how he was gonna start working on our cover story, well and too how he was gonna pack it so full of misinformation that those SangreDenar mercenaries would be chasing

144

their tails for days, maybe weeks, maybe months; and even though that kind of talk from Mike would have worried me before, even though it would have stirred me up good and cautious just a day or two earlier, well now I took a kind of satisfaction in it, reckless satisfaction maybe, but satisfaction just the same: feeling like maybe he'd decided some time in the night that it was all that we could do, our only way to get back at SangreDenar, leastways while we were stuck in Xamon, leastways for the time being. Feeling too like maybe he was right: like maybe feeding the folks at the base some misinformation would help us keep our wits about us, help us keep a lid on things and act like we were none the wiser to SangreDenar; help us make it through the next few days and weeks without wanting to burst out crying, wanting to burst out screaming about everything we knew they'd done.

And me, I figured Mike was most up to the task, I figured that if anybody could think up a story to throw SangreDenar for a loop and send them running in circles it was Mike, being as how he'd always managed to come up with cover stories for us before. Sure, those ones had been your more simple and basic stretches of the truth, rather than out and out fabrications, but still I figured Mike could handle it, once he put his mind to it, so I just left him to it and let myself go somewhere else, to my own kind of sanctuary, my own way of dealing with things. And even though my mind was feeling kind of numb, kind of rubbery, so that truly it was hard to concentrate at all, finally I got into something of a groove, in my own way, and I took to thinking about my guitar: about the feeling of it in my hands, the tingly buzzing of the strings beneath my fingertips whenever I took to playing it; wishing I had it there with me, wondering when I'd get to play it again. Too I was thinking about Digna, hoping she'd found some reporters, hoping that even as we were walking she was convincing them with her smile, and her eyes, and her angling forward, of the need to go to Ochoa, to see everything we had seen there; and a part of me was cursing myself for my shyness, for my never being able to think of what to say or how to say it, and wishing that somehow I'd been able to say something special to her, though I still wasn't sure what that might have been.

But then I took to focusing on my song, my new one, about how I wanted it to start and what I wanted it to sound like, and before long I could almost hear it in my mind, could almost hear each and every high note, each and every mournful chord; and me, I liked it, I liked where it was going and how it was all coming together, and truly I wished I had my guitar right there with me, so I could hear it out loud like I was hearing it in my head, so I could make sure it really was as good as I was thinking it was. And too I got to thinking about lyrics, about words for my song, and seemed to me they'd have to be something out of the ordinary, something a body didn't come across just every day; and first I thought about asking Mike to write me some, being as how he'd always been so much better than me at that kind of thing, being as how it was more in his line, but then I got to thinking on how busy he was gonna be, how occupied he was gonna be thinking us up a good cover story and otherwise trying to keep SangreDenar guessing about what was going on in Xamon. So instead I took to thinking I'd just write some up myself, even if it took some time, even if it made me stretch myself and my mind farther than I ever had before; and I liked that idea, I liked it and thought I'd work on it, even though I knew it would be a challenge, even though I knew this song would have to be better than anything else I'd ever written. Just in case I were to see Digna again, you see, and to play it for her, once I was home, once I was back in a world I recognized as my own. Because I knew if I ever got that chance, if I ever saw her again and played for her, I'd have to play something sweet and majestic and beautiful and strong: something that was sad, but somehow happy too, something that was grand and lofty as the wildest dream or night-thought; but more than anything something that was true, something that nobody--no matter how rich or powerful or connected up through politics--could twist around or deny. Something she could listen to and smile, our own pretty little Xamon song.

To order additional copies of *Xamon Song* by mail, use this form. Please enclose check or money order only, made payable to Global Dialogue Press, and return form to:

Global Dialogue Press
PO Box 1781
Mt. Vernon, IL 62864

Prices are subject to change without notice. This offer is good in the United States only. For information regarding international orders, please write to the above address. This offer is effective February 1, 2006 through December 31, 2007.

To determine your price per book, please use the following bulk discount schedule:

1-4 copies: $10.95 per copy
5-19 copies: $9.45 per copy
20 or more copies: $7.95 per copy

Please send me ____ copies of *Xamon Song*, for a subtotal of: $_____
Shipping and handling (anywhere in U.S.): $ FREE
Illinois residents add 7.25% sales tax: $_____
Amount Enclosed (check or money order only): $_____

Ship my book(s) to: _____

_____

_____

_____